'You're sayin[g] enough?'

'Bingo!' Jacqui said[...] to read minds—esp[...] exist!'

Patric grabbed her arm and hauled her up against him. 'If my mind has become non-existent it's entirely your fault.'

'Let me go!'

Patric drew her lower body up against his own. 'Not until I show you just how explicit I can be...'

Alison Kelly, a self-confessed sports junkie, plays netball, volleyball and touch football, and lives in Australia's Hunter Valley. She has three children and the type of husband women tell their daughters doesn't exist in real life! He's not only a better cook than Alison, but he isn't afraid of vacuum cleaners, washing machines or supermarkets. Which is just as well, otherwise this book would have been written by a starving woman in a pigsty!

Recent titles by the same author:

PROGRESS OF PASSION

DANGEROUS GROUND

BY
ALISON KELLY

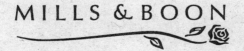

MILLS & BOON

FOR KERRY & MARYANN–
BRILLIANT CRITICS, EVEN BETTER FRIENDS!
THANK YOU

*MILLS & BOON and the Rose Device
are trademarks of the publisher.
Harlequin Mills & Boon Limited,
Eton House, 18-24 Paradise Road, Richmond, Surrey TW9 1SR*

© Alison Kelly 1996

ISBN 0 263 79431 8

*Set in Times Roman 10 on 10¼ pt.
01-9603-61152 C1*

Made and printed in Great Britain

PROLOGUE

JACQUI hung up the phone and opened her diary to the date ten days hence; five appointments had already been deleted.

'Oh, yeah, I'm free for dinner,' she muttered. 'And at this rate probably will be every night for the rest of my life!'

Strange how bleak she felt now that her once constant desire for just two consecutive free days had actually materialised into three weeks without work and an equally blank employment future. The old adage about wishing too hard for something was certainly being proven in this case.

The bottom line was that her career was pretty much over, and while her savings would certainly keep the wolf from the door for months yet, the goal she'd set herself was being snatched away just when it had seemed within reach. Another fifteen months, perhaps only twelve, and she could have retired a winner. Instead...

Not optimistic enough to risk using anything as permanent as ink, she picked up a pencil and wrote:

Dinner: Patric Flanagan—7:30 p.m. at The Dome.

CHAPTER ONE

PATRIC FLANAGAN recognised her the moment she walked into the restaurant, as did all of the other patrons facing the cocktail lounge. Those who weren't quickly turned their heads in response to whispered comments and discreet nudges.

She was one of Australian advertising's greatest successes, yet even without her celebrity status she'd have drawn the appreciative glances. At roughly five-eight Jaclyn Raynor had been too short to scale the heights of catwalk success, but her thigh-length fair hair and Grace Kelly looks had made her a photographer's dream and a cosmetic company's biggest marketing tool.

Tonight, clad in a body-hugging, choker-necked black dress that ended ten inches above her knees, she had every male head in the restaurant almost swivelling off as they strained to follow her leggy blonde progress towards Patric's table.

The reaction confirmed his belief that if he could get Jaclyn to agree to his idea he'd not only establish a name for himself, in the country where his father's had been an icon, but he'd be halfway to fulfilling the fantasies of every Australian male—hell, every man with a pulse!

He rose as his guest neared his table.

'Hi, Patric,' she said, her voice more gravelly than her appearance led one to expect. 'Sorry I'm late, but Friday nights you're at the mercy of the cab companies.'

'No sweat,' he said, waiting until the eager-to-please *maitre'd* could draw out the simple task of seating the model no longer before retaking his own chair. He'd have laid odds that she was late by design, but since it wouldn't serve his cause any good to say so he flashed the forgiving smile expected of him. 'I don't execute beautiful women for being a few minutes late.'

Maybe not, Jacqui thought, but do you have a smile to die for, or what?

She couldn't recall Patric Flanagan making any sort of lasting impression on the one occasion they'd met before, but then his father's funeral had hardly been the place for such things. In fact she'd spoken to him for no longer than it had taken to sob her condolences and to say how much Wade had meant to her. She hadn't expected to hear from Patric again, so his call last week asking her to dinner had been something of a surprise.

Although she would have accepted the invitation simply because it had been issued by Wade's son, it had been Patric's allusion to the fact that the meeting could be financially beneficial to both of them which had really pricked her interest. And it was *that* which was making her blood pump quicker—nothing more. The fact that he was the sexiest male she'd met since . . . since . . . well, in a *long* time had nothing to do with it! It wasn't allowed to because, with luck, she would be working with this guy.

'I presume you have no objections to champagne?'

His question was accompanied by yet another devastating smile, so Jacqui decided that she'd only imagined the undertone of disapproval in it.

'No, I like champagne.' She smiled, wishing she had the nerve to order a beer. In view of her current occupational status it was stupid still to be clinging to the image that the advertising agency which handled the Risque Cosmetic campaigns had created for her.

'So, Jaclyn,' Patric Flanagan said, his eyes roving over her in a way that was both flattering and arousing. 'How was it I was lucky enough to get slotted into your diary on such short notice?'

Again the smile was charm itself, but she sensed that the question was as leading as any that a prosecuting lawyer could have constructed. She decided to keep her cards close to her chest.

'I haven't felt much like socialising since Wade's death, but dinner with his son seemed an appropriate way to end my isolation.'

She paused as the wine waiter arrived and sought Patric's approval of the champagne.

'Better let Ms Raynor do the honours,' Patric told the man. 'I'm strictly a beer and whiskey guy myself.'

Jacqui registered a touch of nostalgia at the description. Automatically she took a sip of the imported champagne, and smiled her satisfaction to the waiter. When he left she directed her gaze into the handsome face of the man opposite her.

'Your taste in alcohol is obviously inherited from your father.' She smiled, silently acknowledging that his dark hair and eyes were also a contribution from his Black Irish ancestry.

'Dad wasn't around enough to be particularly influential one way or another once I reached the legal drinking age.' His response was a tad accusing, but his eyes said that he wouldn't elaborate on the subject.

Lowering her gaze, Jacqui consulted the over-priced menu while puzzling over the conflicting messages this man was sending.

The appreciative look in his eye when she'd first arrived hadn't been imagined—she'd been enduring them from almost every male she'd encountered since the age of fourteen. But Patric Flanagan also seemed to be emitting an active disapproval of her, and she couldn't for the life of her figure out why. On the surface he was being charmingly urbane, yet her senses were picking up an undercurrent of hostility.

Actually her senses were being entirely *too* responsive in other directions as well!

It had been a long time since a man had triggered the interest of her hormones as quickly as this one had. In her world good-looking men weren't exactly a rarity— albeit that the ideal combination of handsomeness *and* availability was reduced somewhat once sexual preference was taken into account—but her instincts told her that Patric Flanagan was as hetero as a male came! Suddenly aware that she was being spoken to, she shut off her libido and switched on her brain.

Patric watched his dinner companion struggling to bring her mind back to the question he'd asked and silently acknowledged that, despite the intelligent light in her blue-grey eyes, Jaclyn Raynor was only a well-orchestrated promotional exercise away from being the clichéd dumb blonde.

Not that it bothered him. He wasn't interested in forming an intellectually based relationship with her, simply a business arrangement. It wouldn't have mattered if she'd had an IQ higher than Einstein's. His own brain recognised the wisdom in avoiding models in general; gut feeling told him to avoid this one in particular.

No sweat, he told himself; for, while he'd have had to be a eunuch not to feel some stirring of sexual interest in a woman as beautiful as Jaclyn Raynor, he was safe from his more basic instincts simply because of his knowledge of her profession.

'Are you ready to order?' he repeated patiently.

'Oh...yes. Yes, I am.'

Jaclyn, he noted, was diligent when it came to her diet, opting for two starters instead of a main meal. Given the way the fabric of her dress moulded the lush curves of her breasts, he had to concede that there was a lot to be said for diligence.

'Work been keeping you pretty busy?' he asked casually.

'Well—er——'

He kept his amusement under control as his guest tried to dance around a direct answer.

'Yes...more or less,' she said, less than convincingly, her fingers worrying the stem of her champagne flute. 'I haven't done any shoots lately, though. I...I was pretty cut up about Wade passing away.'

'Yes,' he said. 'You seemed very distressed at the funeral. You and my father were obviously extremely close.'

'Yes, we were.'

'From what I understand, Dad was quite instrumental in your career.' He noted how her gaze fleetingly wavered at his words, and the way a hint of her perfect teeth momentarily caught at her bottom lip.

'Wade was pretty much the guiding hand behind my success,' she told him.

'And you're missing that...''guiding hand'', aren't you?'

'Wade was more than just a mentor to me.' Patric didn't miss the hint of defiance in her tone. 'He was a friend. It's his friendship I miss more than anything.'

'I'm sure it is.'

Jacqui shot him a speculative look at his words, but his impassive expression again had her wondering if she'd imagined the implication in his tone. She gave him the benefit of the doubt.

'So when are you due to fly back to Canada?' she asked.

'I'm not. I've decided to stay in Australia.'

'For how long?' She hoped the question would lead directly into the reason he'd asked her here. She didn't want to give anything away by appearing too eager.

'Permanently.'

'Really? Wade said you were very successful as a photojournalist in Canada. What's made you decide to move here?'

He shrugged. 'It felt right. I'm Australian, and I've decided it's time I came home.'

She smiled, and for an instant Patric wondered how it would feel to have that smile directed from the pillow next to his own, knowing that it wasn't for the benefit of a camera or an adoring public. Shoving the thought aside, he concentrated on what she was saying.

'You have a——' she frowned '—an *unusual* accent; I can't quite place it. How long have you lived overseas?'

'Sixteen years. The accent's a bit of everything, I suspect. My mother was French-Canadian; when my parents divorced I moved back to Montreal with her. I went to college in the States; then, like everyone does, I spent a couple of years backpacking round Europe.'

'I didn't.'

'You've never been to Europe?' He was surprised.

'I've never backpacked. I saw Europe from catwalks and photographers' studios.'

'I know plenty of people who'd have rather done it your way,' he said.

'Oh, I'm not complaining,' she said quickly. 'It's just that backpacking sounds more exciting.'

'Perhaps, but I can't imagine you doing it.'

'Why not?'

A look that said she shouldn't have to ask was quickly screened with a glib smile.

'It just doesn't gel with the image of the Risque Girl.'

'Appearances can be deceptive, Patric. As a photographer I thought you'd realise that.'

He shrugged. 'Perhaps. But a backpack doesn't have room for a limitless wardrobe and a truck-load of cosmetics.'

His arrogance was such that Jacqui would dearly have loved to tip the ice-bucket over his head, without even bothering to take out the champagne bottle! She resisted the temptation; her career was in enough trouble as it was without the bad publicity such a stunt would generate. She wished that just once she could drop the fabricated public image she'd carried for the last seven years. She would one day, but financially she couldn't afford to do so now.

She was currently unemployed, and if Patric Flanagan was in the position to point her in the direction of some lucrative work, as he'd implied, then she didn't want to burn her bridges before she'd even come to them. If, however, he was full of it, then she'd tell him exactly what she thought of him and blow his misconceptions of *Jaclyn* Raynor to smithereens!

'How old were you when you started modelling?' he asked.

'Fourteen,' she said curtly. Then, reminding herself that she didn't want to alienate the guy, she turned on a megawatt smile. 'My mum and sister entered me in a teenage cover-girl contest without telling me.'

'And you won.'

'I won.'

'Is that when you met my father?'

'No.' It was obvious from his expression that he wanted her to expand, so she did.

'One of the conditions of entry to the contest was agreeing to sign with a particular modelling agency for twelve months; they went belly-up after about four months when the manager was charged in connection with a child-pornography racket.' She shuddered, remembering how some of the kids she'd come to know back then had been vilely exploited.

Patric swore softly. 'You weren't involved?'

'No. I was one of the lucky ones.' She took a sip of her champagne, and the moment she lowered the glass he topped it up again. She kept her amusement to herself and continued speaking. 'If not for Wade, my career might have ended as quickly as it began.'

'History shows it didn't.'

'No. Your father put a portfolio of me together and circulated it to every modelling agency around the world. Although I had offers from both New York and Paris I ended up signing with a Sydney firm.'

He frowned. 'Not exactly the choice most people would have advised. Least of all, I'd have thought, my father.'

'When I was fifteen it was *my* father who carried the most influence! Wade told him he would ruin my career, but Dad wasn't about to let his baby daughter go—and I quote—"flaunting herself in front of a bunch of men on the say-so of some crazy Irishman!"'

Patric watched as some memory lit her face with genuine delight. If the warmth of her smile could increase the pulse-rate in a male as immune to the outward trappings of beauty as he was, what would it do to the unsuspecting? Of course, he'd never previously considered that parental objections might be a stumbling block to his idea.

'Does your father's opinion still figure in your decisions regarding your career?' he asked.

The question implied that he doubted whether she was capable of handling her own affairs, and it irritated the hell out of her! Not least because she'd found herself wondering the exact same thing. She'd landed in a mess when her parents had died, and just when she'd thought she was out of it she'd lost Wade and suddenly faced more problems.

While it was entirely possible that the man opposite might be able to help her find a solution, she wasn't prepared to politely accept his assumption that she was an imbecile.

'This may surprise you, Patric,' she said, 'but I've been making my own decisions for a long time now. So far I haven't made a bad one.'

'At least, not until recently,' he countered knowingly.

'I...I don't know what you're talking about,' she said, but, hearing the lack of conviction in her voice, added more firmly, 'What so-called "bad" decision do you *imagine* I've made?'

'The one that's caused Risque Cosmetics to pull the rug on your contract with them.'

Apprehension froze her body but her mind was racing, trying to ascertain whether he could possibly mean what she feared. He couldn't know! Not yet, surely? Dickson Wagner, Risque's advertising guru and all-round bastard, had told her that he wouldn't yet go public on the firm's decision. Secure in his position as son of the company's owner, he'd 'generously' offered her another week to change her mind—and her morals!

Patric's brown eyes never wavered from her face, and Jacqui found herself swallowing hard. Oh, he knew something, all right. But how much? What if the guy was only fishing? Not wanting to reveal too much, she decided to try calling his bluff.

'I'm not sure where you get your distorted ideas from, Patric, but it's common knowledge in the industry that my contract *expired* right after Wade died. The company, realising I was distressed, have simply deferred negotiations on the new one.'

'Bull,' he said matter-of-factly. 'I happen to know that unless you agree to new terms—*their* new terms,' he emphasised, 'you will no longer be the Risque Girl.'

Damn! Where had he got his information? More importantly, did he have any idea of what the 'new terms' were supposed to be?

'What are these "new terms" you seem to know so much about?'

'Well, Jaclyn——' he lounged back in his chair and linked his fingers behind his head '—I'm not sure exactly...'

The sigh of relief she was about to let go wedged halfway up her windpipe at his next words.

'But I do know you aren't interested in them, since you've had your agent sweating blood trying to line up new clients for you.'

'How...how do you know all this?'

'Trade secret.'

'You aren't in the *trade*,' she pointed out. 'At least, not in this country.'

'True, but being Wade Flanagan's son affords me——' he frowned '—let's say, the advantage of friendships with well-informed insiders.'

'Too bad it doesn't afford you a pleasant personality!'

He laughed with such genuine appreciation that Jacqui was forced to run through mentally what she'd said. To her it still sounded like the insult she'd intended it to be.

'You've a quicker wit than I credited you with,' he complimented her.

She gave him a dry look. 'Somehow that doesn't strike me as a big wrap.'

Grinning, he again went to refill her champagne glass. She covered it with her hand.

'I thought you said you liked champagne?'

'I do, but the only way you're going to get any more of it into me tonight is if you do it intravenously.'

Patric set the bottle aside and sat back. Her immaculately made-up face might, at a casual glance from a distance, have suggested cool serenity, but from his vantage point he easily recognised the determined set of her jaw, could practically *feel* the irritation burning in her thickly lashed blue eyes. Actually they were now more a storm-grey colour than blue.

He wondered what colour they turned when their owner was sweating in the throes of passion. No, he didn't! Lord, where was his mind?

'OK,' he said, determined to cut the crap. 'Let's talk turkey.'

Jacqui resisted saying that no doubt he and turkeys had a lot in common, and merely nodded.

'My information is that for some reason you and Risque are not going to come to terms over a new contract.'

He looked to her for confirmation, but she simply said, 'Go on.'

'Your agent, Garth Lockston, has been trying to line up a new deal for you, but with no luck...' He paused and gave her an expectant look.

'Keep going, Flanagan,' she said, giving nothing away. 'If you win a kewpie doll I'll let you know.'

'My feedback is that seven years as the Risque Girl is proving a career liability for the first time. New clients fear that, regardless of whether you endorse vacuum cleaners, car tyres or designer running shoes, the public will always associate you with Risque Cosmetics, not their product. How am I doing so far?'

He was spot on, but Jacqui had been too close to Wade to be conned by his son. 'I'm still waiting for you to cut to the chase,' she told him flatly.

'In a nutshell,' he said, 'your career is in danger of becoming nothing more than a distant memory.' She knew her face had given her away when he raised an eyebrow and added, 'I believe you owe me a kewpie doll.'

He was grinning like the proverbial Cheshire cat and anger was singeing her bones.

'Well, at least one of us is thrilled about all this!' she snapped. 'What the hell have I ever done to you?' She wasn't interested in getting a response; she barely resisted the urge to throw her drink over him as she leaned across the table. 'You can,' she said, producing a plastic smile for the benefit of any onlookers, 'shove your dinner right up——'

'Uh-uh, Jaclyn. Think of your reputation. Your career.'

'As you so *happily* pointed out, my career doesn't have much longer to run.'

'True, but I've an idea that can change all that. An idea that'll put you into a tax bracket even your accountant has never dreamed of. Of course...' He paused just long enough to be sure that he had her full attention.

'Of course what?' she prodded, wishing that she didn't give a damn.

'If you're not interested...'

She glared at him, wishing that she could afford to pander to her pride and simply tell him to chew glass, wishing that homicide wasn't illegal.

'You know, Flanagan, the world would have been a much better place if your father had been sterile.'

'More wit!' He laughed. 'You aren't quite the dumb blonde I had you pegged as.'

'Yes, I am.' She sighed and pushed her plate aside. 'Otherwise I wouldn't be still sitting here. OK, let's hear how you think you can resurrect my career. And why,' she said pointedly. 'You don't strike me as the altruistic type, so what's in it for you?'

'A chance to establish myself as a top-flight photographer in this country.'

'That's it? Money doesn't come into it, huh?' She didn't have to manufacture the scepticism in her tone.

He shrugged. 'While my idea will be lucrative, it's the recognition I'm most interested in. Which is why I want you. Jaclyn Raynor automatically creates interest that no other model could.'

'But,' she said, pausing to give him a smirk, 'you've just said that my Risque Girl image will be a hindrance no matter what product I take on.'

As smirks went, his left hers for dead.

'Ah, but that's the point, Jaclyn. I don't want you to take on a product endorsement. I want you to *shed* your current image entirely. I want,' he said, 'the centrefold the big boys couldn't get! I want you *naked*.'

CHAPTER TWO

'SO WHAT do you think? Would you do it?' Jacqui asked as her sister Carolyn placed a mug of steaming coffee in front of her.

'No, Jac, but then I'm eight months pregnant! And even if I weren't after two kids already the old boobs aren't quite up to it.'

Jacqui sent her sister a droll look; Caro was not only stunningly attractive but her IQ was in the genius range. 'You know what I mean.'

'Yeah, I do. What I don't know is if you're here because you haven't made up your mind or because you have and want my approval.'

Jacqui couldn't help smiling. Trust Caro to cut straight to the heart of things. 'Half and half,' she said, pausing to munch into a chocolate biscuit. 'The more I think about it, the more I'm tempted. I just don't want to cause you, Phil or the kids any embarrassment.'

'Oh, c'mon! My kids don't know the meaning of the word, so Phil and I have built up immunity to the condition!'

'Simone starts pre-school next year,' Jacqui felt obliged to point out. 'She could cop a lot of flack. And I'd hate to create problems for Phil at work.'

'The chances of anyone connecting the name Jacqui Raynor with Simone Michelini is remote,' her sister said drily. 'And if you do a centrefold the only problem Phil will have is that every guy in the office is going to be hounding him to get you to autograph his copy.'

'I though accountants were supposed to be rigid, upright members of society.'

'They are——'

Both women turned at the arrival of Caro's husband.

'Which is exactly why——' he grinned at Jacqui '—you're becoming an aunt for the third time in as many years.'

She laughed. 'And here I was blaming it on your Italian blood!'

'That too,' Phil said, dipping his wife over his arm Latin-lover-style for a passionate greeting.

'Aaaah! Careful, Phil,' Caro laughed. 'In my condition sensual reaction could cause *contraction*!'

Jacqui smiled. 'Honestly, coming to you two to discuss an issue of moral judgement makes no sense at all. And anyway you'll be tickled pink when I tell you I've got the chance to make enough money to pay off the balance of Dad's debts before the end of the year,' Jacqui told her brother-in-law.

His stunned expression made her smile.

'How?' he asked. 'By my figures the best you could hope for was twelve months! And *that* was assuming Risque renegotiated your contract with a ten per cent increase.' Suddenly his face darkened. 'Hey, that talk about morality earlier... You haven't agreed to Wagner's perverted contractual terms, have you?'

'Oh, for God's sake, Phil!' his wife snapped. 'Of course she hasn't! How could you ask such a dumb question?'

'You're right.' He sighed and looked at Jacqui. 'Sorry. It's just I'd like nothing better than a shot at that bastard's jaw.'

Though the thought of having her six-foot-five tank of a brother-in-law rearrange Dickson's pretty face was a pleasant one, Jacqui too sought to reassure him.

'Relax,' she told him. 'Regardless of how much I need to pay off Dad's debts, I'm not about to prostitute myself to do it.'

There was a moment of silence as everyone sipped their coffee and indulged in their own private thoughts, then Phil spoke. 'Jac, no one expects you to pick up the tab for your father's mistakes. We've been telling you that for five years! Legally you have no obligation to do so.'

'I feel a moral obligation to the people he cheated. I was the reason he got into trouble in the first place.'

'Rubbish!' Caro said. 'Just because Dad had an ego problem that wouldn't let him accept that his daughter could earn more money than he did doesn't mean you're responsible.'

'I *feel* responsible!' Jacqui said, as she had at least a thousand times before. 'And I'm always going to until I know that every shoddy home Dad built is structurally safe!'

'Hell, don't you think the fools who bought his cut-rate sales pitch should shoulder at least some of the financial blame?'

'Their naïvety doesn't make what Dad did right, Phil,' she said. 'He fed off the dreams of the people who bought his houses, and I intend to make sure that if nothing else they get back the money he owed them! And don't either of you...' she paused pointedly '...suggest selling this house again.'

'As if we'd waste our breath,' Caro muttered.

Jacqui conceded a half-smile; their offer and her refusal were par for the course whenever this subject raised its head. Though she appreciated the sentiment, she had no intention of selling off Caro's financial security while there was an alternative.

The house—mausoleum that it was—had been built by their father for their mother, and at the time of their parents' deaths it had been solely in her name. Maria Raynomovski had willed it equally to her two daughters.

Caro, Phil and their two children, Simone and Nicholas, lived in the main house. For privacy and convenience Jaclyn lived in a self-contained flat separated from the house by an enormous garden, swimming-pool and tennis court. The entire complex had been built from the profits of her father's well-intentioned but overly ambitious desire to prove himself a success.

Unfortunately George Raynomovski's venture into the building industry and his subsequent unexpected death had caused a great deal of emotional and financial hardship for his clients. It was Jacqui's intention to make at least monetary recompense.

'Regardless of what anyone else thinks,' she stated firmly, 'I'm going to make sure that every ill-deserved dollar Dad got is paid back. Even if it takes me another five years to do it.'

'Which brings us back to what we were discussing...'

Caro let the sentence dangle, and under her brother-in-law's questioning gaze Jacqui explained. 'I've been offered a deal to do a series of nude photographs. I'm considering it because, as things stand, assignments aren't exactly rolling in.'

Phil frowned. 'You're certain there's no way round Dickson Wagner's smutty blackmail?'

She shook her head. 'He's the owner's son and head of advertising. All he's got to do is show the photographs that that rookie took of me to the board and every one of them is going to agree that I'm too old to head a new campaign.'

'But anyone who saw the photos would surely realise that a four-year-old could do better with an instamatic camera...?' Phil's words died away as she shook her head.

'His other work is first-rate. Who's going to believe my story that he was paid by Wagner to deliberately make me look bad? Besides, the only way Wagner will agree to letting me choose my own photographer is if I crawl into his bed and agree to stay there. I'd sooner sell myself on the streets!'

Caro swore violently. 'The man is pond-scum! Are you sure that no one else is interested? I mean, you're the highest profile model in the country.'

'Sure! And my profile is indelibly stamped "Risque" as far as other companies are concerned. Once your agent dumps you, Caro, the writing is pretty much on the wall,' she said wryly.

'But a centrefold could be the final nail in the coffin,' Phil pointed out. 'Are you sure it's worth the risk?'

Jacqui mentioned the figure that Patric Flanagan had told her was only a conservative estimate. Both Caro and Phil went slack-jawed in amazement.

'You're kidding?' Phil finally managed to gasp.

'My God, Jac!' his wife exclaimed. 'You must look *heaps* better undressed than I remember.'

Jacqui laughed. 'That's only a guestimate, but I'd say it's not far off. I was offered only slightly less a few years ago, but because of the exclusivity clause in my Risque contract it was never an option.'

'Who's making the offer?' Phil asked, nominating the two biggest-selling men's magazines in the world.

'Neither—a freelancer by the name of...' she paused for impact '...Patric Flanagan.'

'Wade's son?' Caro frowned.

'Yep.'

'I thought he lived in Canada.'

'Apparently he's decided to stay in Australia and try to establish his name out here.'

'Well, a few shots of the famous Risque Girl in the altogether will grab everyone's attention if nothing else!' Phil said.

Jacqui nodded.

'Well, if, as I suspect, he tries to get your written agreement that you'll not give a repeat performance for ten or so years, I'd say the money you quoted would be about right.' Jacqui couldn't help smiling at the speed with which Phil donned his cap as her accountant. 'I suppose he intends to sell to the highest bidder?' he queried.

'I'm not sure,' she said. They hadn't got as far as discussing that the other night. In fact Jacqui had been so floored by Patric's proposal that she'd not trusted herself to enter into too detailed a discussion for fear of putting herself at a disadvantage. Wade's first rule when negotiating deals had been 'Do it with a clear mind and never let them see you're keen'.

So she'd feigned only mild interest as Patric had briefly outlined his idea, trying hard not to drool when he'd tossed out what he'd considered to be a feasible financial return from the exercise. If she was honest, some distant part of her brain might fleetingly have suspected such an offer, but nothing more. It was her face most people wanted—well, commercially at least.

She'd coolly told Patric that she'd have to think about it and had received the equally cool response of, 'Do that. But the offer is only good for a week'.

'Jacqui?' Phil was directing a worried look at her. 'You're sure this is on the up and up? I mean just 'cause this bloke is Wade's son doesn't mean he's a nice guy. He could easily be a weirdo or something.'

'Oh, Patric Flanagan might be a chip off the old block in many ways but he isn't *nice* by any stretch of the imagination!' she said drily. 'He's arrogant, rude, patronising, and...let's see...superficial.' She grinned. 'But weird? No, I don't think so.'

Caro smirked over the top of her coffee-cup. 'As I recall from the glimpse I caught of him at Wade's funeral, he's also sinfully sexy.' She quickly patted her husband's hand and added, 'But of course he doesn't hold a candle to you, darling.'

'Oh, ple-e-ease!' Jacqui stood up, rolling her eyes. 'I'm leaving before I throw up!' She carried her empty cup to the sink. 'I only stopped by to make sure that if I decide to do this you two won't be upset.'

'We won't,' Phil told her. 'But remember you'll probably have every do-gooding wowser in the country calling for your blood if you go through with it. They won't know that the motivation behind it is entirely selfless.'

'Don't make me sound noble, Phil——'

'And the hard-core feminists will crucify you too,' Caro added as Jacqui headed for the back door.

'Naturally,' Jacqui muttered. 'Lord, I hate women who tell other women what they should and shouldn't do! The way I see it, the women's movement was about giving us the right to *choose* what we wanted to do— not have us bowing to a dictatorship of our own sex!'

'Save that line for the Press when they start hammering at your door in the middle of the night,' her sister said sagely.

Jacqui knew that neither of them was understating the impact of what would happen if she accepted Patric's offer, but she figured that after living in the limelight for as long as she had she could endure it for a while longer—especially if it would settle her father's debts once and for all.

'Jac——' Phil's voice was gentle '—Caro and I'll back you all the way, you know that.'

She looked at the loving faces of her sister and brother-in-law and smiled, her decision made.

'Then I guess I'd best start thinking about what wording I want in my contract.' She grinned. 'I've got to meet Patric in an hour and give him my decision.'

Jacqui looked at the harsh purple and gold 'For Sale' sign corrupting the sedate elegance of the garden and beautifully restored Federation-style home, its presence a painful reminder that Wade Flanagan was gone.

She climbed from her car and activated the alarm. The metallic blue Honda Prelude was her pride and joy, and even in the low-crime area of suburban Sydney's upper-middle-class Strathfield she wasn't prepared to risk it getting stolen.

Tomorrow she had to go and have the number plates changed. Since she wasn't renewing her contract the company was no longer willing to let her keep the Risque vanity plates, which she'd been using since some advertising minnow had come up with the idea years ago. Not that she cared. Personally she thought them pretentious, but business was business, and for all intents and purposes the company had owned her—at least on the surface.

Actually, doing a centrefold was the ideal way of thumbing her nose at the image which had been manufactured for her. As the Risque Girl she'd been marketed as the immaculately groomed, fashionably clothed, nonpolitical social butterfly. Away from the public eye Jacqui hated wearing make-up, lived in jeans, and liked nothing better than a quiet weekend alone curled up with a thriller.

As for her public persona of being a heartbreaker of legendary proportions—ha! The hundreds of well-known eligible men who'd graced her arm at opening nights and charity balls over the years were, at best, friends; more often than not they had been guys who'd seen her as either a meal ticket or a potential lay. The equally numerous 'mystery hunks' who'd been photographed with her had been either other models or boyfriends of her former agent Garth, who'd been called on to make up the numbers at the last minute.

As she reached the front door she wished she could see into the future and know for certain that she was doing the right thing; she couldn't, but she rang the doorbell anyway...

Patric Flanagan glanced at the clock on the wall—six forty-five; she was fifteen minutes early. She'd been late the other night by design; today she was early because she was desperate for work. He smiled. Jaclyn Raynor wasn't going to say no.

He deliberately took his time walking down the long hallway, and as his fingers closed over the security lock the shrill sound of the bell broke the silence yet again. Consequently he opened the door wearing an uncontrollable grin.

'You're——' The words lodged in his throat, and he checked the cosmetic-free face just to make sure that it wasn't a schoolkid selling raffle tickets door-to-door. Nope, this was Jaclyn Raynor all right—a Jaclyn Raynor he barely recognised.

Her trademark blonde hair was hanging loose, way past the end of her frayed, faded cut-off jeans, and her bare legs were clad in tennis shoes. Forget the shoes! Hell, flesh and blood women just didn't have legs that good! At least, he hadn't thought so until now. He lifted his eyes and they locked on the loose, none-too-concealing black vest-top she wore, and suddenly swallowing saliva seemed to require a doctorate he didn't have.

'I know I'm early,' she said. 'But you are going to let me in anyway, aren't you?'

The sound of her voice jolted him. OK, man, pull yourself together! he told himself. You knew she had a hot bod, otherwise you wouldn't have suggested this idea in the first place.

'Yeah, sure.' He opened the door wider and stood back to let her pass. 'C'mon in. The studio is——'

'I know where it is,' she said, giving him a tight smile and walking down the black- and white-tiled hall with the familiarity of a frequent visitor.

Patric stood motionless for a few seconds before following her, determined to ignore the way her hips and hair swung with each step. What he had to remember was that this woman was all packaging. She made her money trading off her looks and being willing to turn herself into whatever an advertiser wanted her to be.

The other night she'd been the fashionably elegant sophisticate; today, knowing he'd wanted a different image, she'd gone for the unaffected, casually sexy look. Visually the change was effective—OK, breathtaking, he conceded—but experience kept his brain from responding to the woman's looks as lustfully as his body seemed to be.

One of his first freelance assignments had been for the cover of a woman's magazine and he'd spent days wrapping and adorning empty boxes so that they looked like beautiful Christmas gifts. Over the years he'd worked with similar fake props—some had pulses and called themselves models but basically they were the same as those boxes; beneath the pretty packaging there was nothing of substance.

Jacqui had whimsically imagined that she'd feel Wade's presence the moment she entered the house, but it wasn't so. In fact the only unusual sensation she was experiencing was an alarming awareness of an all too *alive* male! Patric Flanagan had the most unnerving effect on her. The other night, dressed in a dinner suit, he'd seemed to have cornered the market in suave sophistication. Yet now, in his current blue-collar guise of jeans and a white T-shirt, charm was superseded by challenge.

Challenges could often be fun; they could also be dangerous. Watching his sexy stride as he moved towards the breakfast bar dividing the kitchen from the rest of the studio, she *knew* he would fall into the latter category.

'I'm having a cup of tea,' he said. 'You want one?'

The curt way in which he tossed the question without looking at her wouldn't have passed as politeness in anyone's book.

'No, thank you,' she responded.

'Best I can do.' He shrugged carelessly. 'I don't keep a stock of champagne.'

She made no comment, because it was hard to talk and bite your tongue at the same time. Honestly, the guy hadn't inherited even a scrap of his father's Irish good humour and friendliness.

The thought of Wade brought a smile to her mouth and a flood of warm memories, compelling her to study her surroundings. She glanced at the collage of photographs mounted on either side of the doorway they'd just come through, at the black vertical blinds screening the opposite wall, which she knew to be totally glass, and the dozens of overhead lights pointed at various angles from criss-crossing exposed beams...

How many hours had she spent in this room in the last ten years? The place was as familiar to her as her own home, and yet for the first time she felt totally ill at ease. She looked towards the kitchen area, met the penetrating gaze of Patric Flanagan, and immediately recognised the reason.

She averted her eyes, determined to ignore the warm heat in her stomach, and moved to the floor-to-ceiling shelves at the end of the room. They were stacked with the hundreds of photo albums that Wade had accumulated over the years. In all the times she'd been coming here she'd only been lucky enough to go through less than a fifth of them.

'What are you going to do with all these?' she asked, gently fingering the spines of several.

'Dad's trophies?' Her head spun around at his disparaging tone and he motioned to the packing crates littering the floor. 'Put them in storage for now. I don't have time to sort through them and there's no way I'm going to have room for them when I move.'

'Why do you call them ''trophies'' like that?' she demanded.

''Cause that's what they are. Some men might keep track of their sexual conquests by putting notches on the bedposts.' He sneered. 'My old man compiled albums.'

'Wade wasn't like that!'

He sent her a smug grin. 'Wasn't he?'

'No!' she insisted. 'He was kind, funny and...and caring. I should know, I saw him practically every day for the last ten years!'

'Perhaps, but I grew up with him.'

'Too bad you didn't grow up *like* him!'

'I worked hard to make sure I didn't.'

'I can't believe you hate him,' she said. 'Wade was like a father to me; he——'

'Yeah?' Patric cut in, moving to stand less than a foot away from her. 'Well, he sure as hell wasn't my idea of what a father should be! And he didn't come within a bee's backside of being a half-decent husband to my mother.'

Jacqui opened her mouth to defend again the man who had been not just her mentor but her friend, but the words died when Patric reduced the space between them to practically nothing and caught her chin. She knew that she should shrug free of his hold but something in the liquid brown depths of his eyes overpowered her ability to do so.

He watched her swallow nervously as his free hand slipped beneath her hair and caressed the back of her neck of its own accord. The softness he found there made him want to taste it almost as much as he wanted to test the texture of her half-parted lips. The intensity of the need surging through him was stronger than he'd ever experienced before, and as her tongue slipped out to moisten those lips he almost groaned aloud.

The knowledge that she knew exactly what she was doing to him was the only thing that gave him the strength to release her and step back.

'Listen, you might have held the record for being his longest-standing lover, sweetheart——' he tilted her chin '—but don't delude yourself that you were his only one. Like I said, I'm not Wade. I don't bed my models, regardless of how tempting they are.' He turned away in response to the whistle of the kettle.

He moved away so quickly that she momentarily thought that her legs wouldn't support her, but in the face of his ironic sneer they served her well. Then again, she was frozen in shock—partly because Patric believed that she and his father had been lovers but mostly because of the turmoil of sensual emotion that his touch and nearness had created within her.

She started shaking from head to foot. It was anger, she told herself, although why she felt like crying was beyond her. Of course, tears were probably a side effect of humiliation. She'd never experienced humiliation before, but, since she'd just stood there willing herself to be kissed by a man whose opinion of her was lower than a snake's belly, she'd certainly felt it now!

She watched him carry a mug of tea over to the glass-topped coffee-table then drop himself into the massive leather armchair his father had always favoured. The action was very like Wade's, but his cold appraisal was light-years from the friendly smiles his father had bestowed on her.

'Let's cut the crap and get down to business,' he said roughly, 'since you've obviously agreed to my proposal.'

His smug certainty rankled. She wished that she was in a position to tell him she wouldn't work with him for three times what he'd offered! But she wasn't, and, distasteful as it might be working with a guy who obviously considered her a tramp, Patric Flanagan—unlike Dickson Wagner at Risqué—had made it clear that sleeping with him *wasn't* a condition of employment. And the sooner she got this job out of the way, the sooner she could pay off her father's debts and go back to being plain old Jacqui Raynomovski. *Then* the only photographs she'd have to pose for would be the ones her sister took at family gatherings.

'C'mon, Jaclyn,' he said. 'Sit down and stop pretending you're having second thoughts about taking the job. We both know that's why you're here.'

'What makes you so sure I'm not here to turn you down?' she asked, miraculously overcoming the urge to slap his smug face. 'How do you know I'm not here to refuse your offer?'

'A no could have been delivered via the phone. Besides which, if you were going to refuse you wouldn't have tried that little seduction act a few minutes ago or——' he paused, again running his eyes over her body '—put the goods so blatantly on display.'

'You swine!' Jacqui grabbed the mug and hurled it and its contents into his lap.

CHAPTER THREE

'OH, SH...OOOT!'

The ceramic mug flew out of Patric's lap, shattering into pieces against the glass top of the coffee-table as he leapt from the chair, steam rising from the damp section of denim clinging to his thighs. Gritting his teeth, he hastily began to remove his jeans.

'You deserved that!' Jacqui shouted, in a desperate attempt to justify her actions. 'You've got no—— Oh, God!' She gasped as a cruel red stain on his thighs was revealed. Reaction to what she'd done manifested itself in tears and trembling. 'I... I...'

She was pushed aside as Patric, clad only in T-shirt and black underpants, raced to the kitchen sink, and she watched mutely as he saturated a teatowel with cold water then held it to the scald. His face showed almost immediate relief and Jacqui's heaved sigh matched it. Good Lord, what had possessed her to do such a thing? Hot tea!

'You,' he said, glaring with outrage, 'are a *bitch*!'

She winced. 'I... I'm sorry. I truly am. But what you said——'

'Lady, if you think the *truth* hurts you ought to be in my shoes right now! You strut your stuff and you've got to expect...'

Strut her stuff! She clenched her fists, fury flaring again under the second barrage of insults.

'You don't go round trying to permanently scar people!' he roared, then cursed and re-wet the towel. 'What's wrong with the usual slap in the face if you want to pretend outrage, huh?' he asked snidely.

Jacqui snapped! 'A slap in the face?' She snatched her bag and car keys from the table. 'I wouldn't dirty my hands touching you!'

Patric smeared a liberal layer of salve on to his thighs. It could have been a lot worse, and he gave thanks that he liked a lot of milk in his tea and had been wearing jeans. Mind you, he thought, it'll be a few days before you're wearing them again.

He swung his bare legs on to the bed and lay back against the pillows. Talk about a fiasco! He'd really screwed up big time!

Someone should have warned him that a model's temperament was in direct proportion to her success. Then again, he of all people should have known; he'd grown up with a classic example of the phenomenon—his mother.

Madelene Cheval Flanagan had been an emotional minefield, and Patric had learned at an early age to detect the first signs of her infamous temper. While her tantrums and hysterics had been legendary, in the international modelling world they had been graciously excused as artistic temperament. Yet as her career had declined jealousy and alcoholism had dragged her behaviour beyond the tolerance of even those closest to her—Wade included.

He sighed, wondering if at this very moment, somewhere in the afterlife, his deceased parents were hurling insults and accusations at one another.

'Dammit, man! This is hardly the time for inane speculation—you've got a major problem on your hands!'

Pushing his fingers through his hair, he contemplated the ceiling. Without a high-profile subject his whole idea fell flat.

Where the hell was he going to find another model with the marketability of Jaclyn Raynor? Answer—nowhere! He'd known that all along, and catching the Risque Girl in the middle of a contractual dispute couldn't have been described as anything but an act of God. Then, just when he'd imagined that the deal was all set to come together, she'd suddenly gone ballistic with a mug of tea and stuffed everything!

Under normal circumstances her outburst would have been enough for him to want to avoid being in the same city as her, much less within striking distance of her throwing arm, but right now he was prepared to work with Satan himself—or, in this case, Satan's *sister*. Despite the woman's obviously precarious grasp on rational behaviour, no other model was going to give him the negotiating leverage he needed to get his project off the ground.

The smart thing to do would be to give her a few days to calm down and approach her again. Patric smiled. A few more days of unemployment and she would be ready to renegotiate. He recognised dollar signs in a woman's eyes when he saw them, and they'd flashed neon in Ms Risque's baby-blues the minute he'd mentioned what he was prepared to pay.

An alarm bell went off in his head and he bolted into a sitting position, wincing as his thighs protested. If she'd agreed to shed her clothes for his lens who was to say she wouldn't do it for somebody else?

It was entirely possible that right this minute she was contemplating approaching one or other of the big boys in pin-up publishing herself. And there was no way that either magazine would knock back the chance of scooping the print world with shots of the luscious Ms Raynor in the raw! Hell, they'd say, 'Exclusive?' in one breath and, 'Name your price!' before drawing the next.

The notion sent him rushing to his chest of drawers in search of clothes. He'd really have to do some heavy grovelling in the next few hours—and grovelling—even the pretend variety—was something he'd never done before...

Patric tried unsuccessfully for several moments to open the wrought-iron gate set in the fortress-like white fence of Jaclyn's Sylvania Waters home before noticing an intercom button. He groaned aloud. Once she knew who it was she'd be more likely to let loose a pack of snarling Dobermanns than let him in, but short of scaling the wall he didn't have much choice. He pushed the button and waited.

On the drive over he'd done a bit of thinking. In all honesty, he'd been out of line with the crack about her flaunting her body—*not* that that excused her for throwing a cup of scalding tea over him! But he was willing to concede that the action hadn't been entirely unprovoked——

'Who is it?' A male voice crackled from the intercom.

Patric decided to err on the side of caution. 'Er...I'm here to see Jaclyn. I was speaking with her earlier...'

The gate swung open and the voice said, 'No problem; come on up to the house.'

So far so good, he thought, following the gravelled path leading to a huge contemporary house of glass and sharp angles. Now all I have to do is get in the front door. The thought had no sooner popped into his head than a guy with a short-cropped haircut and a body like Swarzenegger's appeared at the doorway.

'Can I help you?' he asked, folding muscular forearms with a dagger tattooed on one and a butterfly on the other across his chest.

Patric always made it a habit to work out regularly, and only last night a friend had said that he looked 'fighting fit'. Right about now he wasn't sure that that was going to be good enough.

'I hope so,' he said, flashing a smile. 'I'm here to see Jaclyn.'

'So you said on the intercom, but I didn't catch your name.'

Patric decided that there was only one thing to do—go with guts! 'Flanagan,' he said, extending his right hand. 'Patric Flanagan.'

'Oh, right!' The hulk smiled, moving to grasp his hand. 'Phil Michelini.'

'Hey, nice to meet you, Phil.' The relief in his body was almost overwhelming.

'Jac's round back in the pool,' Michelini told him. 'Use that side-gate, mate.'

'Oh...sure. Thanks.' Breathing easier, he made his way around the side of the house.

Until now he hadn't given Jaclyn's private life any consideration, but now he was speculating—boyfriend? Bodyguard? Both? The guy was in his early forties at the most, so that eliminated the possibility of his being her father. 'Jac' he'd called her, so he was definitely on friendly terms with her. Lucky him—he'd probably never had hot liquid thrown in his lap!

A floodlight illuminated a large rectangle of water artfully disguised as a lake. Against the hum of October's chirping crickets the sound of someone moving through water could be heard. He moved closer, then halted to watch in appreciative silence as a streamlined female form displayed a smooth, fluid freestyle.

He wasn't sure how long he stood observing her, but at some point he found himself counting the laps she completed. When he reached thirty-one he figured it was time to say something, otherwise he would still be there at dawn.

As she approached the end of the pool, and before she had a chance to execute a tumble turn and head back up the other end, he crouched down and called her name. Her stroke slowed and she glided gracefully into the wall, then looked up and let loose with a succinct four-letter expletive.

She tugged off her racing goggles. 'How the hell did you get in here?'

With her long blonde hair completely hidden under a latex swimming-cap the impact of her face was overwhelming; droplets of water sparkled like crystal in the subdued lighting, lending an almost ethereal quality to her flawless skin and perfect bone-structure. Patric felt his body tighten.

'I asked how you got in, Flanagan.'

'Your boyfriend let me in.'

For a split-second Jacqui was lost, but finally the penny dropped. She decided not to correct his misconception about Phil—what was one more amid all the others this man had of her?

'Why?'

'I guess he thought I looked harmless,' he said drily. 'Then again, he's probably aware of the fact you're more than capable of physically defending yourself, regardless.'

Guilt instantly sent her gaze to his legs. In the limited light it was impossible to see how they were after the tea incident, but his firm muscles were beautifully delineated—as were those of his arms, even though his hands were shoved nonchalantly into the pockets of his fashionably baggy shorts. The aura of high-voltage sexuality the man gave off made Jacqui's stomach clench.

'I meant, why the hell are you here?' she snapped, furious with her observations and her body's reaction to them.

'I came to apologise.'

He was in an area of ground where the floodlight barely reached, and its weak efforts to battle with the darkness gave the planes of his handsome face a sculptured look. They almost managed to make him look sincere, too. Almost!

'Oh, *r-r-right*. You're apologising for letting me tip tea over you.'

'I'm apologising for provoking you. It's you who has to apologise for the tea.'

'I already did that.' She said it so matter-of-factly that Patric felt a sudden need to see if the woman was capable of even an atom of concern for anyone's feelings but her own.

'Obviously I must have missed it,' he said, deliberately lifting the leg of his shorts to reveal the raw red area. 'But then pain can short-circuit a guy's hearing.'

'Oh, God! I'm so *sorry*!'

Her words were half gasped, half squeaked, and it
astonished him that the anguish glistening in her eyes
should cause him more discomfort than what, in fact,
was only a mild burn.

'Oh, Lord, *hot tea*! I...I can't believe I did that. I...I
overreacted. I could have done real damage.' Her con-
trite blue eyes sought his. 'Oh, Lord, I'm so very, very
sorry I——'

'Hey,' he cut in, feeling like the world's biggest heel
for milking the injury for more than it was worth. 'It's
not that bad.' She didn't look convinced. 'Really, the
tea wasn't that hot.'

'That doesn't excuse what I did. Have you had a
doctor look at it?' she asked.

'I got it checked out at the local medical centre. They
don't expect there'll be any long-term scarring.'

'Thank God for that!' Again her anguished blue eyes
sought his. 'I really am sorry.'

The desire to console her physically hit him so hard
that he was actually reaching for her before his brain
kicked into gear and stopped him. He wasn't here to
grant her absolution; he was here purely for business
purposes! He needed her as a model in top *physical*
shape—he had no interest in her mental or emotional
guilt-trips! If she was as overcome with regret for her
actions as she seemed then *good*; it might work in his
favour.

She moved towards the steps of the pool and began
to emerge slowly from the water. Patric couldn't look
away.

The sight of her beautifully moulded body forced into
slinky navy Lycra sent his heart-rate into the danger zone
and put his ability to breathe under question. The legs
of the one-piece swimsuit were cut to the waist and exposed a mouthwatering expanse of hip, and a hint of
firm, taut buttock. He could think of one particular international sports magazine which would have killed if
they'd known they'd missed scoring this for their annual
swimsuit edition!

The view was improved even more when she turned and walked to where she'd left her towel a few feet to his right. Too quickly—then again, given the sexual heat cruising through his body, perhaps it was just in time, Patric decided—she wrapped it sarong-style around her.

Again he was forced to congratulate himself on being able to spot quality a mile off. Well, *physical* quality at least, and only when it came to business.

On a personal level his instincts regarding women had proved to be abysmal, although common sense told him that if he ever decided that he wanted to form a permanent relationship with a woman again he was going to have to move beyond his usual business and social circles to find a decent one. If you wanted an exclusive gem you didn't scout retail jewellery outlets.

Using the corner of the towel draping her body to pat the moisture from her face, she turned to him. She was so close that he could see a solitary droplet of water which still clung to her wet, spiked lashes.

'I really am sorry about what happened today,' she said.

'Yeah, well . . . I guess you took what I said the wrong way——'

'Took it the wrong way!' Her eyes flashed fury, and Patric wondered how her remorse could have evaporated so quickly. 'Telling a woman that she's put the goods on display comes under only one heading in my book, Flanagan! *Insults*! And right under that is another you're familiar with—strutting one's stuff!'

Again he witnessed the emotive energy, which hadn't been caught in any photo he'd ever seen of her. Not even his father had managed to harness it on film, and whatever else he thought of his father he acknowledged that he had been a brilliant photographer.

'Nothing to say?' she said with pseudo-sweetness, reminding him of the fact that she was still ticked off with him in a big way, and that it would take some verbal gymnastics to appease her.

'All I meant was that . . .'

'Was that?' she prodded.

'Was that...well, you'd deliberately dressed out of character because you wanted to show me you could shed the sophisticated Risque image.' He smiled, silently congratulating himself on coming up with such a plausible excuse on the spur of the moment.

She raised an eyebrow. 'Is that a fact?'

'Look,' he said. 'I can understand how, being desperate for work, you didn't want to take the risk I'd change my mind——'

'Oh, give me a break!' she cut in.

Once again Patric was forced to acknowledge that despite what he wished to the contrary the woman before him wasn't the type to be fooled by smooth talking.

'If *I'm* the one who so desperately wants to do this shoot, Flanagan, how come *you're* here?'

He gave her what he hoped was a cajoling smile. 'Would you believe I'm a big-hearted guy who wants to give you a break?'

'Not in a million years! You need me, Flanagan,' she said confidently. 'Every bit as much as I need the money.'

'Why?' he asked.

'Because as the Risque—sorry, *ex*-Risque Girl I'm worth more to you than any other model you could get.'

'No, I mean why do you need the money? You've obviously done extremely well over the years.' He waved a hand to indicate the house and grounds. 'A place like this hardly comes cheap.'

Her stance stiffened noticeably. 'You're right. In fact this place has cost more than you'll ever know,' she told him. 'But what I do with my income is my business. Even if I agree to work with you, how I spend what I earn by doing so isn't open to discussion.'

He held her gaze and wondered what personal extravagances—or vices—made her so defensive.

'Relax,' he said, taking a step forward and placing a hand on her arm for fear that she might storm off.

The touch of his hand against the bare flesh of her right arm poured warmth through her entire body, and yet the parts of her skin that he wasn't touching seemed painfully cold. She lifted her head to meet his eyes and suddenly felt as if she'd been gripped by a raging fever.

She lowered her gaze and, finding that his mouth wasn't such a great alternative, quickly focused on the tanned column of his throat. When his other hand came up to rest on her left arm she couldn't think of *anything* except how it would feel to be a consenting adult in the hands of the man standing opposite her.

The notion surprised her. It had been years since she'd experienced even mild sexual awareness of a man, and then *never* anything on this scale. What a damn waste that it had to occur now, with a guy she not only had to work with but whom she didn't like! Considering the hand fate was dealing her lately, if her luck got any better she'd be run over by a bus tomorrow.

'So what about this idea of mine?' His voice intruded into her musings. 'Do we have a deal or not?'

'I'm not sure we could work together, Flanagan,' she told him.

'Why not?' His eyes glittered with amusement. 'Because we're physically attracted to each other?'

Oh, Lord! Jacqui thought. He felt it too! *That* was as scary as it was reassuring. He was looking at her in a way that suggested she wouldn't have been able to diagnose the problem if he hadn't pointed it out, and she'd have loved to come back with a retort such as, Me attracted to you? In your dreams! But she was determined to be adult about this.

She met his glance squarely. 'That's *part* of the reason.'

'So what's the other part?'

'I'm not sure I particularly like you.'

'So?' He shrugged. 'It won't be the first time I've had to work with a woman who didn't like me.'

'Why doesn't that surprise me?'

'Damned if I know,' he said, with a pseudo-innocence that made her roll her eyes heavenward. 'But don't let the sexual thing bother you. I've outgrown one-night stands, and besides, I make it a point never to sleep with anyone my father did.'

Jacqui saw red. 'I never slept with your father, you moron! Wade and I didn't have that kind of relationship! What do I have to do to convince you of that?'

He shrugged again. 'Nothing. I'll take your word for it.'

His easy acceptance of the truth stunned her. 'You will?'

'Sure. But don't get your hopes up; it doesn't change anything. I'm still not going to bed you——'

'*Get my hopes up*!' She almost choked getting the words out. 'I wouldn't sleep with you if we were humanity's last chance of survival!'

'Good, then that solves our problems. Now, is there somewhere we can go and hammer out the details on this?'

Jacqui knew exactly where she wanted to tell him to go, and just enough expletives to do it thoroughly! Mentally she let them all fly—aloud, she said, 'Follow me.'

CHAPTER FOUR

PATRIC had expected them to head in the direction of
the house, but instead Jaclyn led him towards a fenced
tennis court and across the perfectly rolled clay surface.

The lady sure hadn't been worried about a budget
when she'd forked out the money for this place. Not
that it was any of his business, as she'd pointed out, but
speculating on her lifestyle was a hell of a lot more
comfortable than speculating on how she'd perform in
the sack!

'You want to tell me where we're going?' he asked as
they reached a twenty-foot hedge on the extremity of the
limited lighting.

Her only response was to push open a concealed gate
in the hedge and indicate that he should precede her. He
did, and found himself on a small, grassed area facing
what appeared to be a boathouse, albeit an elaborate
one; it had a paved patio and tinted glass sliding doors.

'What's this?' he asked. 'Your office?'

'My office.' She shrugged. 'And my sanctuary.'

Jacqui entered the modernly furnished apartment,
immediately wishing that she'd suggested having this
discussion tomorrow. Dozens of fashion magazines were
scattered both on and under the coffee-table, wrappers
and paper cups from a hamburger franchise were prominently displayed on the small timber table in the dining
nook, and the pile of clothes her niece had been playing
'dress-up' with earlier was dumped on the sofa and
armchair.

'Maid off this week, huh?'

'No,' she said, scooping up the clothes, determined
not to apologise to anyone as judgemental and arrogant

as Patric Flanagan. 'She never comes in on a Thursday. Have a seat while I change.'

She hurried into her room and tossed the armful of clothes on to her papazzan chair. Terrific! Why hadn't she remembered that she'd left the place looking like the backstage area of a fashion show? Of course, if she hadn't been so upset when she'd got back from her earlier encounter with him she wouldn't have. If the place was a pigsty it was his fault! Not that she gave a tinker's cuss what he thought!

She'd have given anything to dive under the shower and rinse the chlorine from her skin and the tension from her shoulders, but she was too conscious of the man in her living-room to do so. Besides, her tension wasn't likely to disappear until *he* did! The sooner the better.

Pulling open her wardrobe, she reached for dry panties and a T-shirt, and shorts too baggy to draw any snide comments about her body. As an afterthought she reached for a bra too. It was bad enough that she was aware of her traitorous body's response to the man without Flanagan knowing it as well.

Lamenting the fact that her brain and her hormones had vastly different tastes in men, she dashed into the adjoining bathroom, splashed fresh water over her face, and gently began to peel off her swimming cap. As she did so the mirror above the sink reflected facial expressions which—unless she happened to jam her hand in a car door during a shoot—would never be caught on film.

Jacqui was counting the days until she could cut the trademark blonde tresses to a more practical length; others might think her thigh-length hair spectacular but she yearned for something manageable.

'Actually,' she told her reflection as she hurriedly brushed her dead straight mane, 'perhaps I'll even try a perm.'

She tried to imagine herself with a short, curly mop and couldn't. She tried to imagine herself posing nude for Patric and felt her pulse start to race. Relax! she commanded her heart silently. So you're a tad nervous

about this. That's natural. But think of the *money*. Think
of what it's going to do.

Determined to stay firmly focused on the positive as-
pects of this assignment, she left the bedroom to face
the biggest negative one, waiting in her living-room...

She found him staring at the cork board adorned by
dozens of black and white photographs.

'Who did them?' he asked.

'Me.'

'*You*?' Amazement registered not just in his voice but
in his face. 'I wasn't aware you worked both sides of
the camera.'

'It's just a hobby. I know my limitations.'

Perhaps, Patric thought, but it was pretty obvious that
she wasn't aware of her capabilities; her skill with a
camera far surpassed that of the average hobbyist. He
again looked at a close-up of a toddler's wide-eyed surprise as a water fountain she was about to drink from
caught her unawares.

'Did Wade encourage your hobby?' he asked.

'He sparked my interest in photography, but if you
mean did he give me lessons—no.' She gave a half-smile.
'Well, not consciously at any rate; but I mentally noted
everything he ever did or said about photography.'

'It paid off. You're good.'

She gave him a droll look. 'Cut the flattery, Flanagan;
I've already agreed to pose for you!'

'Hey, I'm serious. Some of them are really good. I'm
a photographer, I should know.'

'So was Wade, and in his opinion I was *competent*.
So don't try and con me,' she told him.

Patric wanted to say that *he* wasn't the Flanagan who'd
conned her—but why waste his breath? As far as she
was concerned Wade had probably been able to walk on
water.

He looked around the small flat and again found
that his curiosity about Jaclyn Raynor went beyond what
was necessary for them to work together. He wanted it
satisfied regardless.

'What's the story with all this?' He let his gaze roam the room. 'Who's the guy up at the house? Is——?'

'I'm not sure you need to know the ins and outs of my private life, Flanagan,' she interrupted. 'Now, before we start, can I get you a drink?'

'Call me cautious,' he said drily. 'But only if it comes out of the refrigerator.'

'Don't tempt me to discover if you look as good wearing cold liquids as you do hot,' she said, walking to the small, functional kitchen and refusing to acknowledge the smile which had accompanied his words.

'At least you admit that you think I looked good this afternoon. Was that before or after I dropped my jeans?'

Jacqui wasn't sure if it was his tone or the mental picture of him clad only in black underwear and T-shirt, but one of the two caused her to belt her head on the rack of the refrigerator. She swore.

'You OK?' came the amused enquiry from the living-room.

'Fine,' she muttered, rubbing her scalp and wondering how long she'd have to stay crouched in front of the fridge to cool her flaming face. 'Beer, juice or milk?' she yelled.

'Beer sounds good.' The response came from directly behind her. 'Problems?'

'Er—no.' She hurried to her feet and turned around. Not a good move—it brought her face to face with him. He was so close that they were both standing in the wedge of space formed by the opened door of the refrigerator.

'You have beautiful hair,' he said, lifting one side to catch it behind her ear, and in the process brushing his fingers against her cheek. The effect of his knuckles against her skin was such that she half expected the heat she was emitting to defrost the freezer and drown them both.

'Th—thank you,' she stammered. 'I'm thinking of getting it cut. You know, get rid of the Risqué image for good and——'

He frowned. 'Not before my project you don't. You might be blessed with incredible beauty and a body *most* men are floored by, but your hair is your greatest asset.'

'Really? I happen to think it's my personality—but then you'd know nothing about *that*, since you don't have one!' She pushed him aside and shoved a long-necked bottle at his chest. 'Your beer.'

'Thank you,' he said, a wealth of amusement in his voice.

'Glass?' she asked.

He shook his head. 'Oh, getting back to your hair, I... Let's see, how can I put this tactfully...?'

'From what I've seen of you, Flanagan, I doubt if you could put or do anything *tactfully*.'

'In that case I won't bother,' he said. 'But if I'd seen as much of *you* as you've seen of *me* I mightn't have to ask this question; are you a natural blonde? Because if not we could have a colour co-ordination problem during the shoot.'

It wasn't the question which made her angry—she'd had it thrown at her constantly early in her career—no, what ticked her off was that he was being deliberately provocative. She was torn between instinctive rage and economic common sense, but as she formulated her response the burr of the phone that linked directly to the main house filled the room. Thanking God for His timely intervention, she picked it up on the second ring.

'Hi, what's up?' she asked, smiling when Phil's voice explained that he was just checking to see if she wanted him to turn off the pool lights.

'Thanks, but no. Flanagan's still here. We're discussing the shoot details.'

'OK then. Well, goodnight, Jac. Will we see you at breakfast?'

'Breakfast? Any chance of getting it in bed, Phil?'

'Yeah, but not in this lifetime!' came the chuckled response before the line went dead.

The look on Flanagan's face reminded her that he thought Phil was her boyfriend. She smirked, the idea of having a little fun and getting her own back on him appealing. She continued the charade of talking to Phil.

'In that case I'll see you at brekkie.' She paused, then giggled. 'Promises, promises.' Another pause. She was aware of Patric hovering between the kitchen and the living-room, but didn't look at him. 'OK, *Philly*, I'll wake you when I get in. Sweet dreams.' She hung up wearing a stupid grin.

'Now, where were we?' she asked, turning back to Flanagan, who was now sprawled in an armchair. 'Oh, right, my being blonde. I really am a natural, you know——' She slapped her hand against her forehead. 'Darn it! I should have let you check it out with Phil.'

'Forget it!' he snapped. 'I'll take your word for it. Now, as you pointed out, it's getting late, and unless we get down to business you're not going to make your breakfast-date!'

Escaping to the kitchen on the pretext of getting her beer, Jacqui managed to keep her amusement private.

'Let's get one thing straight,' he said when they were seated in the living-room and separated by the now clear coffee-table. 'I want no one prematurely tipping off the Press about this shoot. Timing on this is going to be vital for maximum impact.'

'Fine with me,' she said. 'But how are you going to guarantee that the lab guys who handle the developing won't blab?'

'Easy. I'm going to do everything myself.'

'Tell me exactly how you envisage doing this layout, and I'll see if I have any problems with it. I want it——'

'Don't say it!' He rolled his eyes. 'Let me guess...you want it to be *tasteful*?'

'Don't patronise me, Flanagan,' she said. 'Actually, I was going to say that I want it to be *successful*. Believe me, if I thought for one second that you were entertaining anything pornographic I'd be on the phone and having you blacklisted with every modelling agency in the country.'

She wasn't joking. If there was one thing she couldn't tolerate it was fast-talking photographers who exploited models for personal gain and the gratification of perverts.

'I've never had any time for pornographers, Jaclyn,' he told her. 'But the point is taken.'

'Good,' she said. 'But, be warned, I'll want the whole thing in writing and cleared by my solicitor before you take one shot.'

'I expected as much. But, like I said, I want secrecy on this and I'll be insisting on a clause to that effect. If anything is leaked to the media via you or your legal advisers, I'll sue the backsides off the lot of you.' He pinned her with a spear-like look. 'Understood?'

'Perfectly,' she said sweetly. 'And I'll make sure I have the same clause written into mine.'

He didn't bother to hide his amusement. 'In that case we ought also to include a clause stating that when we do decide to go public we do it together.'

Jacqui wasn't sure that she even wanted to be in the country once the word was out that she'd done a centre-fold, let alone be present at the public announcement. 'That's not necessary,' she said graciously. 'I don't have a problem with you handling that part of it. Providing, of course,' she added, 'you don't turn it into a three-ring circus.'

'Listen, for the money you're getting you're going to be involved with every bit of publicity my PR people think you should be,' he told her. 'And you'll also agree not to do any more skin sessions for at least five years.'

While Jacqui hoped that the money she was going to get from this would mean she'd never have to do *any* type of modelling again, much less another centrefold, his bossy, arrogant attitude stabbed at her streak of perversity.

'I'm twenty-five years old, Flanagan; a five-year restriction will limit my future options. A thirty-year-old isn't going to have much of a chance against nubile young things ten years her junior. I think you're being unreasonable.'

'Tough,' he said flatly.

'Yeah, on my future!'

'Well, then, my advice is stay off the booze, keep out of the sun and get plenty of exercise. You've got good bone-structure, you should hold up OK. If not——' he shrugged '—practise your art of seduction and that sexy pout of yours, and snare yourself a wealthy TV executive. Who knows? It could be the start of a whole *new* career. A pretty woman can make a whole pile of money as a second-rate actress.'

'She can make a "whole pile of money" as a prostitute too; I'm surprised you didn't suggest that!' Jacqui snapped.

Her outrage turned her eyes to the fiery blue of opal and Patric found it incredible that the utter serenity of her facial features could belong to a person with such a passionate and tempestuous personality. It was no secret that the camera adored her, but so far, in the myriad photographs and advertisements he'd seen of her, no photographer had managed to co-ordinate the timing of the shutter with the sudden, unexpected passion that sparked from her eyes. Patric believed that he could. The idea excited him. Dammit, *she* excited him.

Even sitting there in old hiking shorts and a T-shirt big enough to house them both, she was stirring a level of awareness in him that quite frankly should have had him running for the door. Deciding that if he could placate her it might just stop him from hauling her into his arms and kissing her senseless, he said, 'Once my book is released I'm sure——'

'Your *book*?'

He smiled as confusion caused the anger to ebb from her features. 'Yeah. You see, Jaclyn, I'm not planning your average run-of-the-mill pin-up or calendar, here. I'm planning a hard-covered, glossy coffee-table book. I mean, if it worked for Madonna...'

'You want to publish an entire book of nude photos—of *me*?'

'Nope. I want to publish an entire book of Australian landscapes. But I need an angle to generate interest from publishers. *You* are going to be that angle.'

Jacqui sat back and assessed what he'd just told her: she was going to be the bait to hook the publishers.

'In other words I'm just going to be a backdrop.'

'Oh, no,' he said quickly. 'You're going to have to feature quite prominently in the foreground of every shot you're in.'

'But I'm not going to be in every shot, am I? And it's the ones I'm not in that you intend to be the most spectacular.'

'Ah, Jaclyn.' He smirked. 'You underestimate yourself. Where's your self-esteem?'

'Unlike yours, kept in check!' Flanagan wasn't interested in profiling *her*, only *his* skill as a photographer. While the publishers could use the photographs featuring her to flog the books to the curious general public, he believed the quality of the other shots would have the heavyweights of the photographic world beating a path to his door. Whatever he earned through negotiating the deal and royalties would simply be a bonus.

She looked at him and couldn't help smiling; clearly he had a big opinion of himself.

'What part do you find amusing?' he asked, with a frown.

'Your arrogance.'

'You don't think the idea will sell? You doubt my ability as a photographer?'

'Oh, I think the idea will sell,' she said truthfully. Actually, she thought it a stroke of genius, but she wasn't telling him that. 'As for your ability...' She shrugged. 'You're Wade's son, so that must count for something——'

'Judge me on my merits, not my blood lines! The fact I'm Wade's son doesn't come into it!'

It would have been a reasonable request if it hadn't been so heatedly delivered, but Jacqui didn't say so.

'Fine! But I expect equal consideration! Just because you've *assumed* I'm a dumb blonde doesn't mean I am one.'

'So I'm learning.'

He smiled, and the combination of straight white teeth and warm, amused eyes had such a devastating effect on her that she was certain that had she not been seated she'd have swooned. There was no doubt about it—this man's sexual armoury came under the heading of 'Nuclear'. In an effort to avoid total meltdown of her system Jacqui forced her mind back to business.

'What's this Australian landscapes thing you mentioned?' she asked. 'Are we talking places like Katherine Gorge, the Great Barrier Reef——?'

He cut her off. 'No—places like that and Ayers Rock have been done to dea——'

'You mean Uluru.'

'What?'

'Uluru,' she repeated. 'It's not called Ayers Rock any more, it's called Uluru. That's its aboriginal name.'

'Yeah? Shows how long I've been away from home, doesn't it?'

He was about to launch back into his plans for the shoot when he noticed something gold reflecting up from between the arm of his chair and its cushion. It was a cheap, gold-plated identification bracelet—not the kind he'd have expected to belong to the woman opposite him, but it was hers all right. The inscription proved it. It also set his curiosity racing again.

'Flanagan, are you listening to me?'

The impatient tone jolted him from his musings. 'Sorry. What were you saying?'

'It wasn't important, but can we get on with this?' she asked. 'It's getting awfully late.'

'Sure. Where were we?'

'You were explaining the locations for the shoot.'

'Oh, yeah. Right. Well, like I said, most of the well-known Australian landscapes have been overexposed. This time I want to try something different——'

'Such as totally *exposing* me.'

He laughed. 'True. But I also want to focus on some of the less publicised, unravished areas of beauty in Australia.' He met her gaze.

'Don't even think about saying what I know you're thinking,' she warned.

'I wouldn't dream of it,' he lied, amusement creasing his face as he continued. 'Areas such as Ellenbrough Falls in northern NSW, Kangaroo Island off South Australia, various little out-of-the-way spots in Queensland and Victoria——'

'You can't seriously intend to tramp all around the country?'

'Yep. That's exactly what I intend to do.'

'But that'll take ages!' she protested.

'Not your part. I've already selected the areas I want to feature you in. Your commitment to the project shouldn't take more than three or four weeks, tops.'

'But how am I supposed to get to all these remote places? It's not like they're on major airline routes.' She looked even more doubtful. 'And where would I stay? If they aren't established tourist areas it isn't likely that they'll have much in the way of accommodation.'

'True,' he agreed. He could have alleviated her concerns by admitting that he'd intended booking her into the closest top hotel available and having her flown daily to and from the shoot locations by chartered helicopter, but he didn't. The heat of the bracelet in his hand was inspiring an idea so outrageous that it was almost *bizarre*. He wondered if he was really so insane as to be considering it.

He looked at the woman opposite—who, even dressed as she was, seemed to epitomise elegance—looked at her classically perfect features, her clear blue eyes and creamy skin, and decided that he was definitely insane.

He wanted the chance to cut through the veneer, to see if there was anything of the teenage girl who'd apparently called herself Jacko left in the sophisticate who was known as the Risque Girl. He suspected that there was—part of it being the elusive flashes of passion he'd seen, and he wanted that passion on film.

Of course, he'd bet that the only time it surfaced was when the spoilt Ms Raynor was finding things a tad too tough for her, and, while the shoots would be tiring work, air-conditioned luxury hotels and chartered helicopters to and from the locations weren't exactly going to be a hardship for a professional model like her. But what if she *really* had to rough it?

'You might be looking for this,' he said, handing the bracelet to her.

'Oh, thanks!' She took it with embarrassed haste.

'Has it sentimental value?' he asked.

'That's its only value. I got it when I was fifteen.'

'In that case it's lucky I found it.'

'Mmm,' she agreed carelessly.

'Jaclyn,' he said, with assumed casualness, 'are you still keen to try backpacking?'

'Backpacking?' She frowned. 'What, you mean round Europe?'

'No, I'm thinking of something a little closer to home.'

She gave a confused shake of her head. 'I don't get what you mean.'

'It's simple. I was planning to go by four-wheel-drive to the various shoot locations.' He paused, sensing that he was making the biggest mistake of his life. 'How are you at navigating?'

CHAPTER FIVE

JACQUI perched on the edge of one of the chairs which graced the front veranda of the main house, waiting for Patric. She felt like an emotional cocktail which had been shaken with enough force to register eight plus on the Richter scale.

Hardly surprising, she thought, considering everything she'd been through in the last ten days. Not only had she endured endless confrontations with the arrogant Mr Flanagan—both on the phone and face to face—as they'd fought out details regarding their arrangements, but she'd ricocheted from one legal appointment to another.

There had been meetings with her solicitor, Flanagan's solicitor, Flanagan *and* his solicitor and, of course, her solicitor, and with the dozen or so legal eagles that represented Risque Cosmetics—the last in order to end formally her commitment to the company. After all the legal mumbo-jumbo she'd had to study Jacqui felt as if she could have sat for the Bar exam today and passed it! Unfortunately she faced nothing so simple.

She checked her watch; Patric wasn't due for another ten minutes. He'd said 6 a.m., and, if there was anything she'd learned from the myriad meetings they'd had, it was that punctuality was only seconds away from being an obsession with him. Well, she'd learned that *and* the fact that what she was doing to her hormones, by agreeing to accompany him on these safari-like shoots, was probably listed as cruel and inhuman treatment! She only had to be in the same room as him and her pulse started sprinting. Which was damned irritating since she didn't even like him.

Her sigh turned into a yawn. She was dead tired. She'd not finished packing until after midnight, and the moment she'd crawled into bed Mother Nature had staged a rock concert complete with stroboscopic lightning and heavy-metal thunder. Sleep had finally embraced her somewhere between two a.m. and two-thirty, but her alarm had brutally snatched her from its arms only a few hours later.

Hearing a car slow as it neared the house, Jacqui checked her watch—one minute to six. No prizes for guessing who it was swinging into the driveway, but his choice of vehicle caused her to frown.

When Flanagan had told her that he'd purchased a four-wheel-drive vehicle specifically for travelling from one remote shoot location to the next, she'd visualised it as one of the several ritzy Japanese models which had become as common in suburban Sydney as taxis. She certainly hadn't anticipated the very basic, khaki-coloured Jeep-like thing that jerked to a halt in front of her.

She might not know a lot about cars, but she knew enough to know that this one was *old*.

'Good morning,' she said pointedly when, after climbing out, he immediately reached for her luggage without sparing her a glance.

'If you say so,' he grunted.

'I was simply being polite——'

'Don't bother,' he advised. 'It takes more than polished manners to impress me.'

'Really? I'm surprised, since *you're* obviously devoid of them.'

'Look,' he said, then heaved a weary sigh. 'I can do without your sassy comments this early in the day. OK?'

Jacqui didn't have the verbal strength to bother arguing with him, but the look he gave her when she remained silent was a victory in itself. Funny, she'd never previously thought that designer stubble was all that sexy... *Idiot*, she mentally chided, you still don't!

'Careful with this one,' she said, having seen how he'd dumped the three previous pieces of luggage into the vehicle. 'It's got my cameras in it.'

'Oh? Planning on a bit of behind-the-lens work too, are you?'

'If I get the chance. Is that a problem?' she challenged, wishing he'd taken the trouble to shave so that she could have complained about his being late.

'Not as long as it doesn't interfere with your work.'

'It won't,' she said. 'I can assure you that I'm nothing if not professional.'

'Good, because I won't tolerate anything less.' He stood back and motioned towards the passenger door.

'Neither will I, Flanagan,' she shot back, climbing into the Land Rover. 'And remember what it says in our contract—if I don't like any shot of me, it doesn't go public.' She flicked her hair over her shoulders and added, 'I don't care who your father was.'

He closed the door the instant she was seated, and leaned in her window until his face was only inches from hers.

'You know what?' he said.

This close, his eyes had the potential to melt her toes and pretty much every other part of her anatomy; she edged back, her action putting a half-smile on his mouth and a crease in one unshaven creek.

'Wh-what?' Her voice had all but deserted her.

'That's the *nicest* thing you've ever said to me.'

Patric glanced down at the recently installed cassette deck as a loud click coincided with the ejection of the INXS tape which had been playing.

One of his passions was rock music, but after three and a half hours of it he could have used a change of pace. Conversation would have done, but the woman beside him had nodded off within fifteen minutes of their pulling away from her house, and her eyes had remained closed ever since. No doubt, last night having been

Saturday, she'd been partying until late at one of Sydney's expensively trendy nightspots.

He wished that he could blame his own lack of sleep on anything as deliberately self-inflicted as too much socialising, but the truth was that his mind had been too active to recognise his body's need for slumber.

Last night, after double-checking all his gear and packing it into the car, he'd crawled into bed at the very respectable hour of ten-thirty in preparation for his early start.

But every time he'd closed his eyes he'd seen images of Jacqui on the insides of his lids. Yep, *Jacqui*. He hadn't been able to think of her as Jac*lyn* since the night he'd seen the bracelet, and although it had been inscribed Jacko he felt the name too harsh—just as Jaclyn had suddenly seemed too...too fabricated.

Of course, it didn't make a scrap of difference what her name was because *that* wasn't what was causing him problems. It was the intrusive image of the woman! It had happened on and off all week, but last night had been the worst.

The minute his head had hit that pillow there she'd been—Jacqui walking into the restaurant, Jacqui standing at his front door, Jacqui emerging from the swimming-pool, Jacqui trying to back her way into the refrigerator!

At one point he'd sought to relieve the vice-like grip that such visions had on his loins by staring at the ceiling; unfortunately, it had been like switching from a television screen to a movie screen. And cinematography had made Jacqui Raynor's liquid grace and soft-focus beauty the stuff of dreams. Except, dammit, he hadn't been asleep!

The roar of a lorry overtaking him made him glance at his speedo; he was doing only seventy in a hundred-and-ten speed zone.

Annoyed that his concentration was less than it should have been, he mentally shook himself and, without taking his eyes from the road, reached for the case of

cassette tapes sitting on the small seat dividing the driver
from the passenger. An electric shock caused him to
snatch his hand away and glance quickly to his left.

'Sorry,' Jacqui muttered.

She was curled up against the door, with her legs
tucked under her and her impossibly long hair draped
about her like a shawl.

'I thought you were still asleep,' he said inanely,
stunned by the effect her sleep tousled sexiness had on
him. He forced his attention back to the road, determined to ignore her, but he couldn't stop his peripheral
vision noting the movement of her long, sensual fingers
over the spines of the cassettes, or himself wondering
how they would feel sliding over his spine...

'Anything particular you'd like to hear?'

Her words were husky from sex—not sex! He thumped
the steering wheel with his fist. 'Sleep, you idiot! *Sleep!*'

'Don't call me an idiot!' she snapped, punching his
arm.

'No, not you!' he said hastily, mortified that he'd
spoken aloud. 'I meant me! I was talking to myself!
Er...thinking out loud.' Damn it, Flanagan, he thought;
get a grip on your libido!

She gave him a short, questioning look, then swung
her feet off the seat, turning so that her back was to
him. For the next half-hour neither of them spoke, and
the cassette deck remained loudly silent. Patric went from
feeling relieved to uncomfortable to downright guilty,
which was stupid because he hadn't done anything to
feel guilty about!

Spying a service station up ahead, he concluded that
his uncharacteristic edginess was due to nothing more
than a lack of breakfast, and decided to rectify the
problem. He'd be fine once he got some coffee into his
system.

He eased his foot off the accelerator, signalled left
and swung into the garage car park. Still his passenger
made no comment. Rolling into a parking space, he
switched off the ignition and turned to her.

'Jacqui?' She glanced at him and he sent her what he hoped was a placating look. Considering the force behind the punch to his arm, he wanted her calmed down before she got anywhere near hot liquids. 'I'm sorry. I'm not such great company first thing in the morning.'

'From what I've seen so far, Flanagan, the time of day has little to do with it!'

Jacqui quickly escaped from the car, the need to put some distance between herself and her travelling companion suddenly overwhelming. Patric Flanagan was the moodiest damn man she'd ever met, and God knew she'd met plenty! He was——

A loud wail invaded her thoughts at the same instant as someone grabbed her upper arms and hauled her backwards. The driver of the car, passing only millimetres in front of her, hurled a tirade of abuse questioning her vision and intellect.

'Same to you, mate!' she retorted automatically, seconds before the realisation of what had nearly happened dawned. Severely shaken, she offered no resistance when her rescuer turned her trembling body into a comforting embrace.

Her brain, like her heart, was racing. One more mindless stride and she'd have ended up under the car's wheels! She squeezed her eyes against reactive tears and forced herself to take deep, slow breaths. In...out. In...out. In...out...

Her next clear thought was of how good it felt being held like this, being able to rub her cheek against a firm male chest—— Her eyes flew open.

These days blue chambray shirts weren't a rarity, but Jacqui knew, even without looking at the face of the wearer, exactly whose chest she was rubbing against. Her first clue was that her pulse had gone from registering alarm over the near-accident to registering sexual awareness. The second was the deep unusually accented drawl which now met her ear.

'Jacqui, you OK now?'

She lifted her head to look at him. The level of concern she saw in his eyes surprised her. She let her gaze drift to the dark stubble on his jaw, and discovered that the combination of concerned gentleness and hard masculinity did funny things to her insides.

'Jacqui? Are you OK?' he asked again. She smiled, feeling ridiculously thrilled that he'd stopped calling her Jaclyn.

'Yeah, I'm fine.'

'You sure?'

'Certain.'

'Well, be more bloody careful in future!' he said, physically lifting her arms from around his hips. 'I don't fancy working with a model with a tyre-tread embedded on her belly!'

Well! So much for thinking his concern was personal, Jacqui thought, embarrassment at how she'd clung to him surging through her body. Oh, Lord, she wanted to die! Maybe if she laid down in front of the nearest petrol pump the next car driving in would do her the favour of *not* missing.

Suddenly Flanagan's comments about the tyre-tread on her belly prompted her to consider something which had slipped her mind. Oh, no! The Press would really have a field-day with *that*! And she could imagine how caustic Flanagan's comments would be. Good thing she was a dab hand with make-up, because there were some things she wasn't about to bare to anyone.

'C'mon, Jacqui, stop daydreaming!' she was ordered. 'I've planned this trip to a schedule and I don't plan wasting any more time on pit-stops than is absolutely necessary.'

She was tempted to point out that this 'pit stop' had been all his idea, but she didn't. Instead she threw him a snappy salute and, this time checking to see that no cars were coming, scurried across the driveway to the door marked 'Ladies'.

Five minutes later, wearing a baseball cap, and with her hair secured in two long plaits, she entered the café.

After ordering a cup of coffee and two slices of raisin toast she visually scouted the room, trying to spot Flanagan. He wasn't at any of the occupied tables, so she moved to the nearest empty one and sat down.

The raisin toast was a burnt swimming-pool of butter—the way she liked it; the coffee was the instant variety and weak. One out of two wasn't bad. Nibbling the toast, she looked out of the glassed wall beside her at the activity going on in the driveway.

Four leather-clad bikers were grouped around a Ducatti bike, and the concerned looks on their faces told of a major mechanical problem.

Automatically she glanced to where the Land Rover was parked and again she puzzled over its appearance. She'd have expected Flanagan to go for luxury rather than durability and practicality, and as for the trail-bike attached to the back... Well, discovering that he had a penchant for motorbikes was downright scary!

A minibus emblazoned with the name of a junior cricket club opened its doors to let loose a rowdy group of boys and two bedraggled-looking adults, and behind it a tourist coach full of pensioners pulled up. Instantly the noise level in the until now practically empty restaurant rose as the travellers entered. Defensively she turned a little in her seat, putting her back to the growing throng.

While it was unlikely that anyone would recognise her in worn jeans and a plain sleeveless top, with her hair plaited and tucked beneath a cap, it had happened before; Jacqui could just imagine the ribbing she'd get from Patric if his travelling schedule was delayed because she was obliging people with autographs.

'Where's mine?'

She turned, startled by the softly drawled question. 'Pardon?'

'My coffee,' Flanagan said. 'Where is it?'

She pointed to the counter, now concealed by a crowd of elderly people from the tourist bus.

'Ah, swell! Thanks a lot! Why couldn't you have gotten it when you got yours?'

'I didn't think of it,' she replied honestly.

'Do you ever think of anyone but yourself?'

He was being totally unfair, but she couldn't be bothered to waste her breath saying so. 'I'd stop whingeing and queue up if I were you, Flanagan; otherwise you'll jeopardise your precious schedule.'

He moved off, muttering under his breath, unaware of the drooling glances of two teenagers sitting at a nearby table and the double take of a middle-aged waitress filling a serviette dispenser.

Fools, Jacqui thought. You're thinking with your hormones and letting a taut backside, a muscular physique and drop-dead good looks cloud your common sense. The man is a judgemental rat with a bad attitude! And until sex appeal becomes personality, Patric Flanagan won't have one!

About ten minutes later the man in question returned, carrying a tray which held two cups of coffee and a plate of half a dozen doughnuts.

'A hangover from my time in the States,' he explained, sitting down opposite her and pushing one of the steaming coffees towards her.

Jacqui looked from the cup to him.

'Peace offering,' he said. 'I figure we'd best make an effort to get on since we'll practically be living in each other's hip pockets for the next three weeks.'

She gave him a sceptical look. 'That's a lot to expect from one coffee.'

'OK, you can have a doughnut, too.' The grin that followed his words had no trouble in drawing one in return.

No doubt about it, she decided, picking up a sugar-coated ring, good looks and charm had been working for men and against women since time began, and Patric Flanagan had inherited more than his share!

'You sure this won't stuff up your schedule?' she teased.

He grinned. 'The schedule isn't carved in stone.'

'Your father's always was.'

'I told——'

'Yeah, I know,' she interrupted. 'You're not your father.'

'Right.'

'So, how come you hate him so much?'

'I don't hate my father.'

'You could have fooled me.'

'Probably. It sure seems like Wade did.'

'What's that supposed to mean?'

'Just that your blind adoration of the man is based on limited knowledge of him.'

'I'll have you know that Wade and I were extremely close!'

'And this sounds like *we're* extremely close to another argument.' He lifted one eyebrow. 'Want to see how long we can skirt around it?'

She frowned, pretending to give the suggestion deep thought. 'The subject of Wade, or arguments in general?'

'Arguments in general and *specifically* Wade.'

'OK,' she agreed cheerfully. 'And if we can manage that tomorrow we'll try walking on water.'

Amusement sparkled in his eyes. 'Think it'll be *that* hard, huh?'

'Probably.' She grinned. 'Let's face it, Flanagan, our track record pretty much shows that there's no common ground between us.'

He shook his head. 'Not true. The problem isn't *common* ground, it's *dangerous* ground.'

His look challenged her to deny his words. Jacqui took a deep breath, planning to do exactly that, but the intended lie was choked off by the thickness of the atmosphere.

She was unable to look away from his perceptive and penetrating gaze, and the way her blood was warming had nothing to do with anything as innocuous as rage. She wished she could honestly claim that she didn't know what he meant, or at least come up with some witty remark, but she couldn't. And remaining mute wasn't helping the situation any.

'I have a rigid rule of keeping my dealings with photographers strictly professional,' she told him. 'So if you're worried that I'm suddenly going to let my hormones start ruling my brain—don't be.'

'I'm not.'

Well, that makes one of us at least, she thought.

'All I'm saying,' he continued, 'is that the pressure of this...this sexual thing between us is causing us to argue, not the fact that we have nothing in common.'

He helped himself to a doughnut and Jacqui found herself almost groaning as she watched his even white teeth bite into it. What would it feel like to have those same teeth nipping at her bare skin? She closed her eyes against the desire such thoughts provoked, only to open them and realise from his expression that possibly it wasn't the doughnut that he was mentally tasting.

He groaned and ran frustrated fingers through his hair. 'Look, we're adults,' he said firmly. 'And since you readily admit that you're too professional to let an affair complicate your work——'

'Affair!' She hadn't even mentioned the word. She deliberately hadn't mentioned the word!

'—and since, on principle, a model is the last woman I'd ever consider getting personally involved with, I don't think there's any need for us to be so defensive with one another. Why don't——?'

'What's your hang-up with models?' she cut in, wondering why he'd sounded so disparaging towards them.

He opened his mouth to reply, then shut it in the wake of obvious second thoughts.

'Well?'

He frowned. 'Why do you ask? You're not about to launch into a heartfelt defence of the profession, are you?'

He looked so bothered by the idea that she couldn't help smiling. 'No. I'm curious, that's all,' she replied honestly. 'What caused your anti-model attitude—a bad relationship with one? What?'

'Let's just say that I don't want the mother of my children to be a model.'

'But *your* mother was a model.'

'Exactly. And I wouldn't wish my childhood on *any* kid, much less my own.'

'Why?' The line of his mouth told her that he wasn't going to respond. 'Hey, c'mon, Flanagan,' she said good-naturedly. 'Don't stop now; this is as close to a conversation as we've ever got!'

He burst out laughing. The sound was warm and genuine, without even a touch of cynicism.

'You're right,' he said. 'But let's continue it on the road.' He wrapped the remaining four doughnuts in a paper napkin.

Jacqui stood up and picked up her bag. 'OK, but let's grab some munchies from the vending machine before we go,' she said, moving towards the furthest exit, where four confectionery dispensers were.

After fishing almost three dollars in coins out of her purse and feeding them into the machine, she turned to Flanagan and gave him her most beguiling smile. 'Got any change?'

'Sweet tooth, huh?' He shook his head. 'Not a good trait in a model.'

'I'm one of the lucky ones; I don't have a problem with my weight.'

He slid two fingers into the fob pocket of his jeans as he pointedly ran his gaze slowly over her. The combined action seemed incredibly sexy and sensually threatening. Jacqui took a step nearer the machine, trying desperately to concentrate on the various sweets and savoury crisps on offer while attempting to defuse the atmosphere with chatter.

'Of course, I'll never have the elfin-waif look that's so hot on the British and European modelling scene at the moment,' she prattled on, randomly punching numbers on the selection panel.

Peripherally she was aware of Flanagan inserting coins into the machine. He was so close that her denim-clad bottom was brushing against his denim-clad thighs, and she made the scientific breakthrough of recognising denim as a conductor of electricity!

'Er—thanks...er—what's your favourite?' she asked.

'Oh, I'd have to say the thigh-length-blonde-hair-with-plenty-of-curves look,' he said, turning her to face him. 'To hell with Euro fads.'

'I—I meant,' she stammered, her heart pounding, 'what do you like to eat?'

'The same, I think,' he replied, moving closer. 'But let's check to be sure.'

His head started to lower and Jacqui was hypnotised by his approaching mouth. Oh, yes! Oh, no! For a moment desire warred with panic inside her, then his mouth closed over hers and the floor dropped away...

CHAPTER SIX

THE flavour of coffee and sugared doughnut lingering on Patric's mouth and tongue was a thousand times more delicious than when she'd consumed the same only minutes earlier, and Jacqui's response to the strange, new, unnameable hunger gripping her body was to part her lips and feed it. She did . . . and tasted heaven.

The sensations coursing through her body were both exciting and terrifying. Her blood felt as if it was vaporising and her balance was so disrupted that she felt as if she was tumbling off a cliff. Her hands clutched feverishly at the man responsible, but as the tempo of the kiss changed she relaxed, and her fingers slowly inched their way over the chambray-covered firmness of his chest.

Allowing herself to be guided solely by her body's desire, she sought the role of aggressor, and when her tongue slipped deeper between Patric's lips she wasn't sure if the approving groan came from her throat or his. But the ribald remark that followed was definitely from a third party.

'Gee, I thought there were laws against doing it in public!'

Jacqui pulled her head back so quickly that she bashed it against the machine, but under the gaze of the snickering spotty-faced youths embarrassment numbed her to any pain.

Slightly dazed, and afraid that the kiss rather than the knock to the head was the reason, she allowed herself to be propelled outside by Flanagan. Actually, given the grip he had on her forearm, 'allowed' wasn't the right choice of word, and it seemed to Jacqui that they crossed the car park without her feet even touching the ground.

Then again, she thought drily, she hadn't exactly had her feet grounded when they were inside, either!

When he released her and unlocked the Land Rover Jacqui got in without speaking. *He* didn't need to—the vicious way he slammed her door said volumes!

Head bent, she buckled her seatbelt with a concentration that would have done a heart-transplant surgeon proud, although, considering the way her hands were shaking, any patient she might have got near would have woken up in the morgue, not Post Op! Oh, great, Flanagan! she thought, rubbing her forehead. You've turned me into a crazy person! Even my mind is quaking!

She sighed. OK, it hadn't been entirely his fault. *She* could have stopped the kiss. *She* could have pushed him away. And she would have, except that . . . except that—— Oh, darn! She wanted to cry almost as much as she felt like screaming, which was ludicrous! For heaven's sake, it had only been a kiss. A kiss wasn't the end of the world. So why was she reacting as if it was?

She looked at her still trembling hands and sighed. Because, she admitted dejectedly, for the first time in her life she'd been confronted with raw desire.

Despite the heavily overcast sky she began rummaging through her bag for her sunglasses. She wasn't taking any chances. Sometimes her eyes gave away too damn much, and the last thing she needed was to alert Flanagan to the fact that she'd been vulnerable to his kiss. She gritted her teeth. She didn't want to think about the kiss, its cause, or her response to it any more. She wanted to ignore it. And she darn well would! As of now it was wiped from her brain!

Of course, the effects it had had on her body might take a little longer to subside . . .

Patric gunned the engine to life and swung back on to the expressway, not trusting himself to speak. He was so angry that he wanted to spit. How could he have done that? How could he have been so damn stupid as to have succumbed to his most basic instincts? What had happened to him that he'd suddenly started to keep his brains below his belt, huh? Geez, he'd acted like an oversexed sixteen-year-old. *Worse*!

He shot a look at his travelling companion; she was huddled up against the door with her back turned as much against him as her seatbelt would allow. The only way that she could have put any more distance between them would have been to climb out of the window.

Of course, back at the gas station she'd sure seemed more interested in reducing the distance between them than increasing it! And oh, Lord, he thought, remembering how her body had been pressed into his, heaven should feel that great!

He ran his tongue over his teeth and felt his body harden as he picked up the lingering taste of her. He muffled a groan. Where had she learned to kiss like that? As soon as he'd asked himself the question a picture of Phil Michelini flashed into his mind; jealousy knifed through him with a ferocity he'd have thought impossible.

Cursing, he grabbed a cassette, shoved it in the tape deck and turned the volume up, silently daring his passenger to complain. She didn't.

For the next three plus hours, as soon as one tape finished Jacqui replaced it with another. Thus far Patric had made no objection to her choices, but then, since his collection consisted entirely of hardcore rock 'n' roll, it wasn't as if she could pick a style he didn't like. Actually his taste in music had surprised her a little; she'd have picked him as being more inclined towards what she called mainstream music.

Her stomach grumbled and she decided that if she put off speaking to him any longer she'd starve to death.

'Can we stop and get some lunch soon?' she asked, not looking at him.

'What?' He practically had to yell to be heard over George Thoroughgood and the Destroyers.

She leaned over and turned down the volume. 'I said can we stop for lunch soon?'

'Why?'

She gave him the scathing look he deserved. 'Because I'm *hungry*.'

He sighed. 'Look, we'll be there in another hour or so. Can't you wait until then?'

'No, I can't wait.'

'Well, eat some of those crisps and stuff you bought.'

'I can't.'

He looked at her. 'Why not?'

'Because I left them in the machine.'

'How did you do a stupid——?' He aborted the question as the answer dawned simultaneously with a look from Jacqui which would, he suspected, have killed a more sensitive man. 'OK. OK. We'll stop at the first place that looks like it sells food.'

'Thank you,' she said sweetly.

'But we eat in the car,' he said. 'I want to make the hotel where we're staying early enough to unpack the car and check out the locations I've got in mind.'

Considering the rain, which fluctuated between steady and torrential every twenty or so minutes, Jacqui didn't like his chances, but she didn't say so. And, as they swung off the Pacific Highway in the direction of Wauchope, she couldn't help thinking that they'd both have been a whole lot better off if Patric had chosen a naval navigator to pose for him.

In the wake of their verbal exchange and the lower volume of the music, the atmosphere in the car began to take on the consistency of marshmallow. Jacqui tried to pretend interest in the rain-soaked countryside, but it didn't help. She *hated* his obviously civil silence—it was too forced, too plastic, too…awkward. And, for heaven's sake, they had to work together! What was he going to do for the next three weeks—give her directions in *letters*?

'Don't you think it's about time you quit pouting?'

Jacqui started at the sound of his voice, then sighed heavily. Great, she thought, nothing like starting an assignment all wound up! Of course, working with Flanagan she'd probably end up with her nerves stretched tighter than the Centre Court's net at Wimbledon.

'I'm not pouting, Flanagan. I never pout.'

'*All* models pout. It's second nature to them.' His tone was one of absolute knowledge and disapproval.

She turned in the seat to glare at him. 'You know what your biggest problem is, Flanagan?'

'I should—I'm sitting next to it,' he said drily. 'But no doubt you'll recognise it as something else.'

She continued as if he hadn't spoken. 'Your problem is that you think you know everything there is to know about models because your mother was one and your father spent his life photographing them. You——'

'Let's not forget *bedding* them,' he interrupted. 'The old man was no slouch at that either.'

'So what?' she demanded. 'There's no need to keep going on about it, is there? Or——' she raised a knowing eyebrow '—is that what bothers you—fear that you won't be able to compete with him on that level?' she sneered.

He shot her a furious look. 'I told you my interest in models is strictly professional!'

'You couldn't prove it by me!' she countered, immediately wishing that she hadn't.

'Wrong, lady! That's *exactly* how I will prove it!' He jammed on the brakes and killed the ignition. 'You can bet what happened this morning *won't* be repeated.'

'Too right it won't!' she agreed.

'But, just for the record,' he said, moving to catch her chin with his hand, '*if* your ten-year relationship with my father was as platonic as you make out——' his eyes moved to her mouth as he gently brushed his thumb over her bottom lip '—then I'm already setting a much faster pace than Wade did.'

He withdrew his hand, but his touch lingered, permeating deep inside her. She was incapable of looking away. She swallowed hard, her body warming under the intensity of his gaze. Never had she wanted so badly to be touched.

He muttered under his breath and ran a weary hand through his hair. 'OK, what do you want?'

She blinked. 'Wh-what do I want?' Her voice scarcely registered as a whisper.

He gave her a look of utter frustration. 'A burger, sandwich—what?'

He pointed towards the side of the road. Only then was she aware that they had stopped outside a small general store, advertising hot take-away food. Silently calling herself every kind of idiot, she fumbled first for her handbag and then with the seatbelt.

'No.' The touch of his hand against her shoulder lasted only a second, but its effect sizzled through her blood for much longer. 'Just tell me what you want and I'll get it. It's pouring out there; no point in us both getting drenched.'

The rain was about as close to a cold shower as she could get right now and, brother, did she need to cool off! She thought about arguing the point with him, but decided against it; even professional fighters took a break between bouts.

'Er—thanks,' she mumbled, looking everywhere but at him. 'Um—I'll have a hamburger with cheese and bacon, and a chocolate milkshake.'

Still avoiding eye contact, she held a five-dollar note out to him.

'I'll get it,' he said, reaching for the doorhandle.

'What's this?' she asked, curiously lifting her head. 'Another peace offering?'

He shrugged noncommittally. 'Something like that.'

She offered a tentative smile. 'Flanagan, if you're going to buy me food every time we argue, I'll end up looking like the side of a house.'

'Hmm!' he grunted. 'More likely I'll end up flat broke!'

Watching him dart through the rain to the shop, Jacqui doubted whether he even knew the meaning of the word. Guys who wore genuine Rolexes rarely did.

The final stage of the trip was short and passed peacefully—only, Patric decided, because his travelling companion had been too busy feeding her face to speak. But all good things had to end, and as he stopped outside their destination words tumbled from Jacqui's lips.

'This is where we're staying?'

'Yeah,' he replied. 'It's been restored since I came up here on vacation a few years back.'

She turned from her perusal of the hotel to him, her blue eyes wide. 'You came here for a vacation? From Canada?'

'Well, it was a kind of working holiday,' he qualified. 'I already had the idea for a shoot of out-of-the-way Australian beauty spots, so I started to scout out a few whenever the chance arose. This area was perfect.'

'Well, it's certainly out of the way.' She cast another apprehensive look at the hotel.

Patric didn't know why her reaction made him angry— he'd expected it—but it did.

'Just be grateful you aren't staying in a tent!' he snapped. 'This situation could be a lot worse, believe me.'

'Only if you tell me you have a twin brother who's meeting us here.'

The sarcasm in her tone triggered thoughts of murder in his head, while her lipstick-free lips ignited sensations of passion in him from the neck down. To quell the temptation to haul her into his arms and kiss her senseless, he concentrated on the lesser of the two evils— homicide.

Given the fact that this woman would have tried the patience of a celibate saint, let alone a mortal male, he figured a male jury would return a verdict of justifiable homicide. Of course, the way his luck was going, he'd end up with a jury of hardcore feminists—or, worse, models! Swell, just what he needed—more models!

He gripped the steering wheel. 'Jacqui,' he muttered through clenched teeth, 'get out and start checking in while I unload our gear.'

'Rest assured, you'll get clean rooms and good, no-frills meals in the dining-rooms, but this isn't like them city hotels, Ms Raynor,' advised the buxom, middle-aged woman who'd finally responded to the reception bell which Jacqui had rung a dozen times. 'There's no room service, and if you want to make a phone call you'll have to use one of the public phones. There's one in the main bar and another in the dining-room.'

Under the woman's penetrating gaze Jacqui felt obliged to respond. 'I...er—that's fine.' Her smile was ignored and the lecture—at least, that was what it seemed like—continued.

'There's eight rooms and four bathrooms. Usually you'd have to share a bathroom with the occupants of one of the other rooms, but we only have one other guest at the moment so you won't have to worry.' She paused and glared over Jacqui's shoulder.

Following the woman's gaze, Jacqui turned to the doorway, which was now almost totally blocked by Flanagan. He held a suitcase in each hand, a duffle bag under each arm and a third over one shoulder. Any other man would have looked clumsy and overloaded carrying so much, but Flanagan moved into the room with his usual ease and grace and systematically lowered each item to the floor.

'Afternoon, I'm Patric Flanagan.' His outstretched hand was ignored.

'You didn't request *two* rooms when you phoned, Mr Flanagan,' she accused him in the tone of a teacher to a particularly wayward student.

'That's because I wasn't originally expecting to need two,' he explained reasonably. 'I'm sorry, it slipped my mind to notify you about the second. Is that a problem?'

'Fortunately for you, Mr Flanagan, we aren't heavily booked at the moment, but, as I said to Ms Raynor here, we could have been.'

'Guess we're lucky we didn't arrive here at the same time as you had an international conference going on, huh?' The smile he flashed had probably managed to worm him into the good books of granite-hearted women before today, but Jacqui almost cheered as the formidable hotelier simply gave him a droll look.

'Will you be paying for both rooms, Mr Flanagan?' she went on. 'Or should I have separate accounts?'

'Charge everything to me.'

'May I see some identification, please?'

'These do?' He presented his driver's licence and credit card to her.

A *gold* card, Jacqui noted. But if the woman was impressed it wasn't enough to make her tone any friendlier.

'The dining-room is open between six-thirty and eight-thirty. Bar closes at eleven every night except Sundays, when we shut at ten.' She lifted overly pencilled eyebrows. 'And if you have any complaints——'

'I'll speak with Jack Reagan, the owner, about them,' Patric cut in smoothly, in a tone of subtle warning.

'Oh, I'm sure there'll be no need for that!' She forced a smile that didn't reach her eyes. 'Now, here are your keys, Mr Flanagan.' The woman pushed them across the counter. 'I'll fetch my husband to help take up your bags.' With that she vanished into the adjoining bar.

'How long have you known the owner?' Jacqui asked.

'I don't. I read his name on that licence over there.' He nodded to the wall. 'I'm not in the mood to handle *her* attitude too.'

'That makes two of us,' she muttered, picking up her key. 'You sure don't get this kind of treatment at the Hilton.'

His expression was condescending. 'Must come as a shock to find that not everyone is impressed by meeting the famous Risque Girl.'

'Actually, Flanagan,' she said haughtily, 'it comes as a welcome relief!'

Jacqui's room was clean, and furnished with a well-maintained pine wardrobe, double bed, side-table and a chest of drawers. A portable TV sat on top of the chest of drawers and an uncomfortable-looking armchair kept guard over the French door leading on to the upper veranda.

Clean, cosy and practical, all it needed was a few posters of pop stars from the early eighties and it would have been nearly identical to the room she'd had as a kid.

She glanced at the luggage by the front door, then sighed. Nope, it could wait. Taking a shower and grabbing a nap were light-years ahead of unpacking in her schedule of priorities. Perhaps once she'd rid herself of her travelling fatigue she could start dealing with the cold sweats which started every time she thought about the fast approaching photo sessions and the reality of what she was going to do—a nude shoot!

Jacqui entered the bathroom from her room, locked the door in the opposite wall, which connected to another room, and stripped off her clothes. Then, after regulating the water temperature, she stepped eagerly into the shower. Ah, bliss!

She let the warm water relax the muscles across the back of her shoulders for several minutes, then slowly started to rotate them. Ouch! The sudden movement of her head provided physical proof that Flanagan really was a proverbial pain in the neck!

Lifting a hand to knead the protesting muscle, she warned herself not to think of the man. Ha! He was the whole reason she was here.

She squeezed a liberal amount of her favourite shower gel into her palm and began soaping it over her body. Her nudity brought her mind back to the shoot. For the first time the monetary rewards and the fact that she'd once and for all be rid of her father's debts didn't seem like a good enough reason for what she was going to have to go through.

She knew that legally it was way too late to decide that she'd changed her mind, but she had all the same. Exactly when, she wasn't certain, but at this moment she'd have given almost anything to be able to walk away from the whole thing—especially the photographer involved.

Not for anything as reasonable as moral reasons, but for utterly irrational ones. Not because she didn't think Patric would be strictly professional at all times, but because she wasn't sure *she* could be. Not because she doubted Flanagan's skill as a photographer, but because she *didn't*!

A good photographer could capture the very soul of his subject and lay it bare, and, from what she'd seen of Flanagan's work, he'd progressed beyond being just good years ago! What worried her wasn't so much the thought that strangers would see her naked exterior, but that *he* would see her naked interior. Patric Flanagan might be making her feel all the things she'd always hoped she would, but the last person she wanted to be feeling them for was him!

Why did fate have such a warped sense of humour that her heart should pound and her breath should catch at the sight of a guy she could barely tolerate and who actively disliked her? Why did liquid sensuality dampen her body the moment his muddy brown eyes locked with hers?

Why couldn't he have been ugly, or at least gay, instead of being the most drop-dead gorgeous heterosexual male she'd ever met? Why couldn't his kiss have been repulsive and oppressive, instead of bone-melting and spiritually freeing? Why couldn't his touch have been rough and chilling, instead of caressing and warm? And ... and why the hell couldn't she even analyse the whole stupid situation without lust burning her insides and sending her nipples rigid?

Cursing, she shut off the hot water and turned the cold tap full on. With luck she'd get pneumonia and have to be hospitalised. Two seconds later, deciding that she wasn't tough enough to endure the freezing spray any longer, Jacqui stepped from the shower and went on to Plan B—praying that it would rain for the rest of her life!

CHAPTER SEVEN

PATRIC sipped his beer and waited as his opponent surveyed the snooker table. After four days of rain the locals assured him that it was finally gone. With luck they could scout locations tomorrow and start shooting the next day.

His gaze drifted to where Jacqui and three adoring local teenage boys were playing a game on a video machine.

They'd hardly spoken since their arrival and Patric suspected that she was making as much effort to avoid him as he was her. Each morning she was finishing her breakfast by the time he arrived down to have his, and the situation was reversed at dinner. What she did during the day he had no idea, since he'd spent the last three days burning up his excess energies and boredom by throwing his trail-bike through the mud a few miles out of town.

On the occasions that they were in the bar at the same time she was usually holding court with various admirers of both sexes, while he had to endure hearing continual accolades about how wonderful she was.

On cue, his middle-aged opponent spoke. 'She's so flamin' *nice*. Not a bit hoity-toity like you'd expect.'

'You had your shot?' Patric returned.

'Yep. Pocketed the last red, but missed the yella.'

Patric nodded and leaned over the green felt table, lining up the yellow. He sank it and then proceeded to do the same to the green and brown balls. Unfortunately when sinking the brown he hadn't hit the cue ball exactly right, and as a result his shot of the blue was more difficult than he'd planned. He took his time studying the best angle and was finally about to make his play when——

'You should have put more return on the white ball, Flanagan.'

Barely managing to stop himself from miscuing, he turned around to face a solicitous-looking Jacqui.

'I *know* that. Now, if you'll keep quiet——'

'I really think you'd be better off playing the blue from——'

'Don't you have anything better to do? Where are your pals?'

'They've gone to the bar. I told them that you and I'd have a game of doubles against them when you finished here.'

'Did you, now?'

'Yeah.' She placed her money on the rim of the table to reserve it. 'But, given your last shot, I'm beginning to think I should have picked another partner.'

Patric turned, sank the two remaining coloured balls with more flourish than was necessary, then sent the black off all four cushions before pocketing it.

He laid his cue on the table and faced her. Her hair was pulled back and she'd actually tied a knot in it just below her neck. She wore faded jeans, fashionably ripped at both knees, and an oversized man's shirt tied at the waist. On her, the plainness of the outfit was both elegant and wild, but, experiencing a tightening of *his* jeans, he didn't risk speculating about whether the tantalising hint of skin and navel the get-up exposed was intentional or not.

He fixed his gaze on her face, biting down a groan as a cheeky smile curved her lush mouth and lit the depths of her eyes.

'Not bad, Flanagan,' she said. 'Where'd you learn to play snooker?'

'Dad bought me a table for my eleventh birthday. I used to spend hours in the games-room practising trick shots.' He folded his arms. 'From what you said before, so did you.'

'We didn't have a games-room, much less a pool table.' She picked up the cue he'd discarded and checked its weight against the one she already held.

'So where *did* you learn to play?' he asked when she began chalking the cue he'd favoured.

'The Ashfield Pool Room.'

'*A pool hall?*' He couldn't begin to imagine her in a pool hall. 'Jaclyn Raynor actually went into a pool hall?'

'No.' Her laugh was full of genuine amusement at the notion. 'But Jacqui Raynomovski used to hang out there from the time she was ten.'

Even if he hadn't been slack-jawed with shock he still wouldn't have had a chance to respond to this unexpected information, because two of the youngsters she'd been with earlier approached, carrying large glasses of beer.

'What do you say to twenty bucks, Jacqui?' one asked.

'I say let's make it fifty.'

'You're on!'

After his first three shots Patric decided that they'd have more chance of winning the game if Jacqui racked her cue right now! Not that she couldn't play—hell, she was the one who'd scored all their points so far—but the sight of her denim-clad bottom bent over the table every time she lined up a shot was playing havoc with his concentration.

He moved to the other side of the table only to discover that from this side, whenever she leaned over, the front of her loose-fitting shirt dipped to display a teasing shadow of cleavage.

Patric closed his eyes in frustration, but a second later opened them as waves of jealousy surged through him. Hell, he probably wasn't the only male in the place aware of the scenery. He cast a look at the guy standing next to him and fought down the urge to put his fist into his gut. Oh, sure, the guy *looked* like he was only interested in the game that was going on, but who'd buy *that* story? It wasn't——

'Hey, Flanagan!' Jacqui's impatient voice cut through his musings. 'It's your shot.'

'Huh? Oh, right. We're on the green——'

'No, Flanagan, Pete just pocketed the green.' She gave him a weary look. 'Get with the programme, will you?'

Cursing himself for being so distracted that he'd lost track of the game, he rechalked his cue as he studied the lay of the balls. For all intents and purposes he was snookered, with the brown ball tucked in behind the black and the pink.

Determination not to allow his mind to be sabotaged by his feminine partner prompted him to choose the riskier of two possible plays. Instead of merely going for the safe option of playing off the cushion and nudging the ball away from the hole, he decided to play the white ball hard off the cushion, so it would cut behind the black and pink and, hopefully, slice the designated brown ball into the top left-hand pocket.

It was a tough shot, but by pulling it off he'd prove that once he set his mind to it he was immune to the distractive powers of the woman opposite.

Leaning low over the table, he spread his legs to balance himself and looked along the line of the cue, easing it between his thumb and forefinger—once, twice...

He watched the white ball ricochet off the cushion at speed, but the rest seemed to be in slow motion... It passed the black with less than a hair's width to spare, hitting the edge of the brown and rolling it towards the pocket. Its momentum slowed to snail's pace, and for long seconds it teetered on the extremity of the felt.

Patric sucked air through clenched teeth and closed his eyes until a flat-sounding clunk told him that the ball had dropped into the pocket.

The congratulations and accolades of those watching were inconsequential in the face of his relief at having exorcised himself. He lifted his gaze to Jacqui, intending to give her a smug grin, but the idea died the instant he realised that her delighted smile was meant for *him*. He was still seeing the wide grin and the sparkle of admiration in his mind as he took his next shot and screwed it up completely, leaving Pete's partner with the opportunity to clear the table.

By some miracle the guy muffed it, and Jacqui had only three simple shots for victory. She made the first two and then, to the utter disbelief of everyone watching, she hit the white ball too hard, causing it to ricochet off the black into the side-pocket.

'Oh, darn!' she wailed. 'I can't believe I did that!' She bestowed a dazzling smile on the two teenagers they'd been playing. 'Guess that means we owe you fifty, huh?'

'Say, you want to play for double or nothing?' one challenged, his words bringing a look of horror to his mate's face.

Patric, not eager to put his body through more trauma, didn't give Jacqui a chance to open her mouth.

'Not tonight, mate,' he said, pulling a fifty-dollar bill from his wallet and handing it to the guy who'd looked as reluctant as he himself felt about a rematch. 'We have to get an early start in the morning.'

Jacqui's eyes were questioning as they met his.

'Rain's cleared,' he said simply.

The teenagers muttered farewells and left them.

'S-s-so we start shooting...tomorrow?' Jacqui looked apprehensive. 'Won't it still be too...too wet?'

'Probably, but that's no reason not to pick out the locations for the next day. We've wasted enough time already.'

She nodded and looked at her trainer-clad feet. 'What exactly do you have in mind for me?'

Patric almost groaned at her choice of words.

'I mean, you haven't really told me——'

'I never plan my photographs in advance. I prefer to wing it,' he said. 'To go with my feelings at the time—understand?'

'Yes, but...' She seemed unable to stand still, shifting her weight from one foot to the other, then shrugging and sliding her hands into the back pockets of her jeans. The action pulled the shirt tighter and lifted her breasts.

'Look, Jacqui, I'm bushed,' he said, although fatigue was the least of his worries! If the arousal stirring in his body increased any more, going with his feelings would mean that Jacqui would be spread beneath him on the snooker table. What had happened at the gas station had only proved that an audience was no safeguard against his libido. He disguised the beginnings of a groan as a sigh. 'Can't this conversation wait until tomorrow?'

She nodded. 'Sure. What time will——?'

In his haste to escape he anticipated her question. 'We'll leave after breakfast.' With that he strode off in the direction of the stairs, intent on a very cold shower.

Three times Jacqui lifted her hand to knock on Flanagan's door, and three times she dropped it back to her side. She was so appalled by her timidity that on the fourth attempt her determination not to chicken out resulted in her almost hammering down the door.

It was whipped open with a rough, 'What the hell——?' and suddenly she found herself confronted by a bare-chested Flanagan. 'Good God, Jacqui, there's no need to pound the thing down! I thought it was the vice squad.'

Did the vice squad arrest people for being sinfully sexy and spectacularly proportioned? she wondered. Because, if so, Flanagan had good reason to be looking concerned. His muscular chest was covered with a smattering of curling, dark hair, which still held droplets of moisture and thinned into a V as it arrowed down over a flat stomach and into half-zipped jeans.

She swallowed hard, forcing her eyes back to what she considered was the much safer region of his face, only to find herself mesmerised by a drop of water which tumbled from the end of a curl below his ear, down on to his shoulder and along the line of his clavicle.

'What's up?' he asked.

My pulse-rate, she moaned silently, wondering if she could speak without panting. 'Oh—er——' No panting, but she was pretty squeaky. She tried again. 'I need to know how early "after breakfast" means. I... well, I don't want to...' Drat the guy! Couldn't he have put on a shirt or something? 'I don't want to sleep in.'

He raised a sceptical eyebrow. 'As I recall, you're the first up in the morning.'

'Er—well, yes. I just thought you might want to get a *really* early start—like seven or six or...' The way he was watching her was jumbling her brain. 'Or...earlier.'

His only response was to run a hand through his hair and then shake his head. A stray droplet landed on her cheek. Given the heat coursing through her, she was surprised that it didn't evaporate on contact. Instead Flanagan lifted a gentle hand to brush it away, then, smiling absently, he continued to stroke his thumb over her cheekbone. Beneath his touch she froze to the point where even her lungs wouldn't work.

'You have the most incredibly soft skin. It looks and feels like whipped cream.'

Maybe, she thought frantically, but inside she felt like hot fudge. His touch moved to her lower lip, and Jacqui thought that she swayed a little before his eyes trapped hers, making her mind incapable of registering anything but the number of times he traced her mouth. One, two, five, eleven ...

'Eight!' he rasped.

'E-e-eight?' she stammered, steadying herself on the doorjamb as he stepped back suddenly.

'Yes, meet me in the dining-room at 8 a.m. sharp!'

Confused by his sudden switch of moods, she blinked, and when her lashes opened she was facing his closed door.

'You want to tell me why you threw that snooker game last night?'

The question was asked with casual uninterest as Flanagan snapped off several quick shots of a fast-running stream, but Jacqui wasn't deceived.

'What makes you think I threw it?'

'Your previous shots showed that you're too good a player to have gone in off the black on such an easy play.' He lowered his camera and looked at her.

'Look, one of the kids was desperate for money to buy his girlfriend a birthday present. All right?' she asked tersely. 'If you're bothered about losing a few bucks deduct it from my fee.'

'I intend to.'

She rolled her eyes, and was horrified to hear the camera whirr to life as she did so.

'You rat! I told you no candid shots and I meant it!' Her outrage only made him laugh and he stepped back, accomplishing another two shots in the process. 'Your face is so *expressive*! I love it——' His fingers stilled on the camera only milliseconds before the entire world froze around them.

Afraid he'd hear the pounding of her heart in the stillness, Jacqui heaved in a less than steady breath and rushed into speech. 'Try *that* again, Flanagan, and you'll find my *vocabulary's* very expressive too!'

He grinned. 'I imagine it must be if you spent your tender years hanging around pool halls. What's the story? I had you pegged as a well-brought-up private-school girl, from a cashed-up blue-blood family.'

She burst out laughing. The reality of her childhood was so removed from what he perceived it to have been that she wasn't sure if the tears in her eyes sprang from regret or mirth. Immediately she tugged the peak of her baseball cap further over her face; it was OK for *her* to question her reaction, but she didn't want him doing it.

'A joke that funny should be shared,' he said.

She blinked until her vision cleared, then shook her head. 'I think it would lose a lot in the telling.'

'Why not tell me over lunch and let me decide?'

The tone of his voice and the way he was looking at her told her that interest rather than curiosity had prompted the request, and ten minutes later she sat cross-legged on a blanket, sharing not just cold chicken and salad with him, but a large chunk of herself.

'I grew up in Dulwich Hill, Sydney. My folks came to Australia from Poland in the fifties. They were both only seventeen, with very little money and about as much education. Dad worked for a few years with the railways, then was lured to the Snowy Mountains to work on the Hydro-Electric Scheme in the hope of better money.'

'A lot of immigrants worked there—my Irish god-father included.' He smiled. 'And we're both first-generation Australians; seems like we've found some of that common ground we talked about the other day.'

They both knew that it was what he'd called 'dangerous ground' which had dominated their conversation five days ago, and that it was becoming more and more difficult to ignore. She could tell by his eyes that he was waiting for her to contradict him.

She pursed her mouth, knowing that to retaliate would be to open a Pandora's box. It was amusing to know that she could read him so easily, but her arrogance evaporated when the notion that he might be equally attuned to *her* thoughts burned into her brain.

'Our backgrounds are light-years apart, Flanagan,' she said, determined to respond only to what he'd actually said.

'You don't know mine well enough to know that.'

'Your father told me enough about his life for me to know you didn't grow up with parents who had to scrimp and save to make ends meet. And no son of Wade's would have attended an overcrowded state school or worn hand-me-down uniforms.' She grinned. 'And I'm damn certain you didn't cut school in——'

'No chance,' he broke in. 'I went to boarding-school.'

'Wade sent you to boarding-school *that* young?' She was appalled that any parent would do such a thing.

'I'm talking about *high* school,' he stated, then frowned. 'Aren't you?' She shook her head. 'You mean you played truant when you were only in primary school?'

'Yep. By high school I was averaging at least two days AWOL out of every five!' She laughed at his open-mouthed horror. 'How else was I going to learn to play pool?'

'God, Jacqui! What was wrong with your parents?'

'Nothing!' she snapped. 'They *sent* me to school; I just didn't *go*. It's not like they could handcuff me to a desk! Why do people always blame the parents when a kid bucks the system? School *bored* me. I hated it and got out as soon as I was old enough!'

'But... but you're so bright, so——'

'Yeah, right. That's what all my teachers said, and Lord knows how many social workers! But back then there weren't programmes like the ones they have these days for gifted and talented kids. Nobody knew what to do with me. It was OK for my older sister, Caro; she was comfortable being a perfect straight A student but I wasn't.

'When she and Mum heard about the teenage cover-girl contest, they figured it would be the best way to get me out of both school and the crowd I was hanging around with.'

Patric leaned back on his elbows. 'And did it?'

'Eventually.' She laughed. 'But the upshot of the whole thing was that Caro fell for one of the bikers I was hanging around with.'

'You ran with a bike gang?' He stared at her with disbelief. 'You're making this up, right?'

'They weren't exactly a bike gang in the true sense of the word,' she admitted. 'But they weren't choirboys either.' A flood of memories brought a smile to her mouth. 'It all seems a billion years ago,' she said wistfully. 'Every one of them is probably a fine, upstanding citizen now, with kids of his own.'

She was silent for a few minutes as, one after another, faces from her past were projected on to her mind. She sighed. 'I thought about having a huge reunion party a few years ago, but decided against it.'

'Considering what a headline like RISQUÉ GIRL EX-BIKER MOLL would have done to your career, I'm not surprised.'

Jacqui spun her head round to face him. 'I didn't scrap the idea of a reunion because I thought it would hurt my modelling career!' she said hotly. 'I was worried that the old crowd would think I was doing it all for pose value. You know—showing off.'

'You continue to surprise me,' he said. 'First I discover you were immune to my father's charms——'

She opened her mouth, intending to defend Wade, but he continued before she could get a word out.

'Then you turn out to be just three breaks short of a professional pool hustler——'

Jacqui couldn't help laughing at his phrasing.

'And now you tell me that not only were you a rebellious, wilful brat but that you knocked around with the type of guys most people cross the street to avoid——'

'They weren't *that* bad.'

'And, to top it all off, you worry about them being offended by your success.' He shook his head. 'You don't fit the archetype of a model.'

'That's because there isn't one. Contrary to what you believe, models aren't simply one huge commodity. Modelling is something we *do*, not who we *are*.'

His eyes flashed scepticism. He opened his mouth then shut it, as if thinking better of what he'd been about to say. But Jacqui wanted to know.

'What?' she prompted.

'Forget it. Let's——'

'No,' she said firmly. 'Tell me.'

'OK,' he agreed. He narrowed those intense brown eyes of his on her. 'Why did you decide to take this assignment?'

If she'd thought for one moment that telling him about her father would have made him offer to tear up the contract they'd signed and let her out of the deal, she would have. But Patric Flanagan was his father's son and, as such, he'd hardly be likely to let sentiment or nobility stand in the way of a business deal. Her problems were her own and nobody else's, and she intended to keep them that way.

'I had my reasons,' she said finally.

He gave her a disappointed look. 'Not good enough, Jacqui. You insisted on my asking you the question; I insist on an honest answer.'

'I wasn't happy with the conditions of the Risque deal.' Now, there was an understatement. 'I might have grown up on the wrong side of the tracks but I know my own worth.'

'Not enough money, huh?'

She disguised a shudder at the thought of Dickson Wagner's disgusting proposition with a derisive laugh. 'Not *nearly* enough!'

He studied her in silence for several moments, then stood up and started packing up their lunch things.

'Wrong side of the tracks or otherwise, Jacqui, you sure learned your trade well. Congratulations,' he said. 'You're a model all right. Through and through.'

His tone moulded the words of praise into an insult.

'C'mon,' he said, when she remained sitting. 'Lunch-break's over!'

CHAPTER EIGHT

By THE end of the afternoon Patric had selected the two sites where he wanted to photograph Jacqui the next day. One was a small clump of rocks in the middle of the creek, and the other was a vast expanse of land covered only with long, sun-bleached grass. Which was a damned sight more than she'd have covering her! Jacqui thought as they pulled into the hotel car park.

The butterflies in her stomach had long fled—chased away by the dinosaurs which currently resided there. She glanced across at the man beside her. Perhaps if she threw up all over him she could convince him that she had some terrible illness, and that if she didn't front tomorrow it would be because she'd died during the night. Ha! If her luck was that good she'd have already won the lottery twice.

'You getting out, or are you planning on sitting there all night?' he asked.

Since lunch their limited conversation had been strictly professional. Flanagan had been thorough in the extreme and, unlike some photographers whom Jacqui had worked with, not the least bit condescending when discussing the angles and light conditions he wanted to use.

When she'd produced her own camera and taken some shots he hadn't made any disparaging remarks as Wade often had about 'amateurs playing artists'. Then again, such would have counted as *personal* conversation, and it was plain that he'd been avoiding that, cutting her short every time she'd tried to start one.

Now, judging by his curt voice, the tenseness in his handsome face and the grim line of his mouth, he wasn't in any mood to hear that she was suffering a life-threatening case of nerves. Sighing, she climbed from the Land Rover.

Patric watched her silent departure. All day he'd had to battle to keep his eyes from straying to her shapely bare legs and the tantalising curve of her behind beneath the khaki hiking shorts she wore. But now, as she walked away from him towards the hotel, he leaned against the bonnet of the car and allowed himself the luxury of looking—secure in the knowledge that these surroundings provided a brake on his self-control that the isolated countryside didn't.

He frowned. The tan hiking boots on her feet didn't give her stride the same jauntiness as they had this morning. Sure, they'd done a bit of walking, but not *that* much. And from the way her shoulders drooped, a person would think she'd spent the day hauling sacks of bricks—or the problems of the world up Everest.

He straightened. Was something bothering her? Nah! Besides, as long as it didn't affect her work, why should it matter to him? And it *didn't* matter to him. Not a bit.

'OK, Jacqui, what's up?'

He'd knocked once and announced himself. She'd been slow to open her door and he'd thought that she might be asleep, but though the bed behind her was rumpled it was still fully made and the room lit by lamplight.

' "Up"?' she echoed.

Her blue eyes were duller than he liked to see them and her face strained. Her hair was loose, and its mid-thigh length matched the hem of her Garfield nightshirt. His pulse and respiratory rates weren't comfortable with the sight of so much smooth, bare leg so he quickly averted his eyes.

'Mind if I come in?' he asked, wondering how she could manage to look both surprised and hesitant at the same time. She glanced down at what she wore and, apparently deciding that it was decent, stepped back and motioned him inside.

Her room was identical to his own, right down to the yellow electric jug and cheap china cups sitting on the small corner-table.

'Any chance of a cup of coffee?' he mused aloud.

'Been banned from the dining-room, have you?' she asked, taking the jug into the bathroom to fill it.

'The dining-room shut a half-hour ago. Which is why I'm here,' he said. 'You didn't have dinner tonight.'

One look at the only chair in the room told him that it would be every bit as uncomfortable as the one in his room, so he chose to sit on the bed.

She returned to the room, set the jug back on the table and turned it on. 'I wasn't hungry.'

'A reasonable explanation,' he conceded. 'Except I've seen you eat. If you're off your feed there has to be something wrong.'

'Not necessarily.'

'You haven't been out of your room since we arrived back this afternoon. Are you sick?'

A moment passed before she said, 'No.'

'So what's wrong?'

'Why does anything have to be wrong, Flanagan?'

'Because you look like hell.'

'Worried I'll mess up your photographs tomorrow? Well, don't be, I'm a whiz with make-up. Remember, I've learned my trade well.' She poured the boiling water into two mugs and stirred the contents. 'Sugar?'

'No, thanks.'

She handed him a cup from arm's length.

'Is that what this is all about—your sulking?'

'I told you, Flanagan, I don't sulk.'

'No, you told me you didn't pout.'

She blinked as if he'd startled her by recalling their conversation so precisely. To be honest, it annoyed him that he did, but as she carried her cup past him to the vacant chair the subtly perfumed scent of her replaced irritation with a more earthy emotion.

The TV was on but no sound came from it, which made the silence between them more pronounced. He got up and turned it off.

'Take over, why don't you, Flanagan?' came the dry response to his action.

'OK, maybe you weren't sulking before I got here, but unless you're a lip-reader you sure weren't watching television.' He returned to the edge of the bed and leaned towards her, his arms on his knees. 'Something's bothering you, Jacqui,' he said softly. 'What is it?'

She gave him a pointed look.

'Besides me.' He smiled. 'If I was your major problem you'd have already kicked me out.'

'Maybe I'm still weighing up the advantage of booting your behind through the window over booting it through the door and down the stairs,' she suggested.

Why not? he thought; he'd sure spent enough time thinking about *her* taut little behind today. And, given the way the soft cotton of her nightdress clung to all her other attributes, this was the *last* place he needed to be!

'In that case——' he pushed himself to his feet '—I'll solve your problem and just——'

'No!' Her hand darted out to grab his arm. Just as quickly she drew it back. 'I need to ask you some questions about tomorrow's shoot.'

Her voice wasn't quite steady, and discomfort shadowed her usually bright face. Seeing her so vulnerable sparked an emotion in him that Patric didn't want to examine too carefully.

'Nervous, huh?' He offered a half-smile.

She sighed, then nodded. 'I'm telling myself it's just another shoot. The same as thousands I've done...' Her voice trailed off and the smile she gave didn't quite work. 'It's stupid, but I don't feel mentally ready for this. I'm not sure I can distance the real me from the professional me.'

Her expression begged him to understand what she was trying to say.

'Is that what you usually do?' he asked. 'Close off your genuine emotions and switch on what you think the camera wants?'

She gave him a funny look. 'Of course. That's why it's called posing.' She laughed, then grabbed her hair and twisted it roughly on to the top of her head and held it there. 'See?' she said, assuming a haughty expression. 'The regal look.' She let the hair fall, tousled it with her fingers, then widened her eyes and wrinkled her nose. 'The girl-next-door look.'

Warming to her task, she sprang to her feet, tossed her head forward once to give her hair a windblown effect, then, lifting one arm, she draped it dreamily across her head and wriggled until the neck of the nightie slipped off her other shoulder. Finally she licked her lips and nibbled her bottom lip. 'This is the seductive-stroke-siren look.'

She giggled and dropped the pose. 'You think I'm an idiot, right?'

'No,' he said huskily. 'I think you're absolutely beautiful.' Before he could talk himself out of it he reached for her and pulled so that they both fell backwards across the bed.

It happened in an instant, and yet Jacqui saw and felt everything in slow motion....

Off balance both physically and mentally, she seemed to free-fall through space into Flanagan's arms, to land across the firmness of his chest. She was winded, not by the force of contact with him, but from the thumping impact of her heart against her lungs and ribcage.

She was intensely aware of every individual change in her body's normal functions—from the increased speed of the blood in her arteries to the way the sensual juices building within her tranquillised her fraught nerves.

But she was equally alert to the feel of the man beneath her, alert to the burning heat coming from his hands as, tangled in her hair, they moved with delirious intensity across her shoulders, the small of her back, her buttocks, and then retraced their path.

Through all this her focus remained on the male face drawing nearer and nearer—the lightly shadowed jaw, the high-ridged cheekbones, and the moist, parted lips, showing a hint of even white teeth and promising pleasure. This was Flanagan—arrogant, conceited, bossy, professional, don't-compare-me-with-my-father Patric Flanagan. And she wanted his kiss more than she wanted to breathe.

Her stomach dipped as if on a rollercoaster as a denim-clad leg moved between hers to flip her on to her back. Her eyes closed at the sound of a resigned groan, but who it came from she didn't know—for she was instantly lost in the taste of passion.

His tongue made one feverish pass over her lips before plunging between them to engage her own in a desire-provoked duel. Recalling how shabbily fate had treated her in the past, Jacqui's hands immediately grasped at his head to guarantee that he wasn't snatched away. She wanted this man more achingly than she'd ever wanted anything—*needed* him, body and soul.

His mouth moved to trail along her neck and she arched into him, trembling in anticipation as she felt his denim-covered arousal against her thigh. She moaned wantonly, totally enmeshed in desire, and when he lifted his head to look at her she knew that what she felt wasn't unique. As he slipped a hand beneath the hem of her nightie his eyes fixed on her face, the silent query in them more than audible, and so erotically exciting that a spasm of need tightened her pelvic muscles.

Jacqui knew that only he was capable of satisfying the sensual hunger gripping her body, for he had triggered it.

When? A minute ago? A week ago? She couldn't say exactly, but she'd endured the famine too long to deny herself the feast. So, like his question, her response was similarly wordless; she flicked off the lamp and reached for his belt. And as their vision adjusted to the darkness nothing more articulate than half-groaned, half-muttered 'mmm's, 'aah's and 'yes'es broke the passion-choked atmosphere of the room as they abandoned themselves totally to each other.

Jacqui marvelled at the mastery of Patric's hands as time after time they stroked the length of her body, teasing, soothing and preparing the path he ultimately took with his mouth and tongue. Her flesh singed and burned under the fire of his touch, inflaming her blood until she could no more have stopped herself from orally worshipping every inch of his body than she could have spontaneously explained how to split an atom.

She'd never cared for science at school, but now she wondered how she'd ever survived without the chemistry she felt in Flanagan's arms.

Patric's greatest fear was that he would be burnt to ash by Jacqui's passion before he could release her from it. No woman had ever before posed a threat to his control as quickly or as effectively as she did. He wanted her fast and all at once, yet at the same time his hands and mouth wanted to savour her inch by deliciously slow inch.

His hands closed over the weighty firmness of her breasts and demanded that his mouth taste their sweet, pebbled peaks. His lips, needing no second bidding, obediently obliged. And as he gloried in the taste of her he heard her pleasured moan through the tips of his fingers as they flattened themselves against the silky muscles of her belly; again his lips greedily followed.

She clutched at his hair when he finally reached her core, and the symphony of her abandoned whimpers as she bent her legs to embrace him made his heart stop. He was shaking as he kissed a trail back to the ardour of her mouth, but that was nothing compared to the quakes of emotion which rocked through him when she demanded the same intimate access to his body that he'd had to hers.

Afraid that the searing desire would be drawn from him before he'd experienced what he craved most—the ultimate possession of her—he closed his hands on a thick strand of the blonde hair draping his stomach and wound it around until her head lifted from him. His chest momentarily cramped at the sight of her eyes clouded in passion and her face flushed with it. No woman had ever looked more beautiful.

She smiled then and, groaning, he levered himself from the pillows to taste that smile. When her eager mouth met his he felt the intensity of his own feelings returned in her kiss. A kiss that went on and on and on...

They were slick with sweat and their breathing laboured when finally he moved over her. He tried, with the remnants of the control he still had, to delay the moment, but she gave him no chance, lifting her hips to meet his thrust.

Jacqui Raynor was something else!

But when their passions simultaneously combusted, leaving him in a glow of galactic brilliance, on some level of his euphoric, clouded mind he suspected that she was much more than that...

Patric squeezed his eyes shut—not against the glare of the morning sun, but against the recognition of his own stupidity.

In sleep the woman beside him snuggled closer, and again his eyes were drawn to her right hip. Again the memory of the man who'd introduced himself to Patric on the front veranda of Jacqui's home sprang to his mind. Only this time the image of Phil Michelini was entirely blurred except for the tattoo of a butterfly on his forearm. A miniature replica of that butterfly was tattooed on Jacqui's hip.

The woman he'd made exquisite love with last night wore another man's brand!

CHAPTER NINE

HE WAS gone. It was morning and Patric was gone.

In the few seconds it took Jacqui to open her eyes and register these facts a million confused emotions attacked her. Yet she didn't need to see the indented pillow next to her to know that last night hadn't been a dream—the slight discomfort in her lower body was infinitely conclusive.

She smiled, wondering if Flanagan had woken to the same sense of euphoric rightness about what had happened.

She frowned, figuring that if that was the case the least he could have done would have been to hang around and share the moment with her.

She sighed, uncertain whether his absence made her feel angry, disappointed or relieved.

'Oh, heck,' she moaned. 'What am I supposed to make of things now?'

What, she wondered, was Flanagan making of things? Of her? Did he consider last night a mistake? Was that why he'd left before she'd awoken? Or was he simply being tactful and giving her time to reappraise the situation? She laughed. Tact wasn't one of Flanagan's strong points! He was handsome, confident, incredibly talented and a fabulous lover, but definitely *not* tactful! And—she sobered—definitely *not here*.

A look at the clock radio told her that he was probably at breakfast, waiting for her to join him. But damn! What was she supposed to do when she did—calmly order tea and toast and make no reference to the evening until he did? Or jump right in and announce that she'd never experienced anyone like him in her entire life?

By twenty-five most women had presumably dealt with at least one 'next morning' scene, but a less than memorable first time hadn't encouraged Jacqui towards an active sex life. Until last night hers had been a case of once bitten—not again! But, while her practical experience was minimal, to Jacqui waking up naked next to the person you'd spent the night with seemed a whole lot more natural—not to mention romantic—than confronting him again fully clothed over a breakfast-table.

'Hey, you were wonderful!' sounded way better than, 'Hey you were wonderful; pass the Vegemite, please.' But then, what did she know?

'You were right, Mum,' she conceded aloud, climbing from the bed. 'The day *has* come when I regret not spending more time at school—they probably covered this situation in sex education class!'

He was sitting drinking his coffee when she reached the door of the dining-room, and if the sight of him made her heart somersault then it made it do cartwheels when his gaze met hers.

She tried to look composed as she started towards his table, but her nerves were such that she wasn't sure if her legs would get her there, and she was teetering midway into the room when he rose and strode to meet her.

'Good, you're up. You've got fifteen minutes to eat breakfast and then we're out of here. I don't want to waste a minute today.'

Though stunned by his curtness, it was the impersonal way he took hold of her chin and inspected her face which made her heart crumple.

'Great, no make-up. I want the natural look.' He released his hold and dipped his head closer. 'But for God's sake camouflage that damn tattoo you've got. It looks cheap.'

He didn't add the words 'like you', but Jacqui heard them in his tone. She didn't bother to try and defend herself against his insinuation for a number of reasons:

one, because she was afraid she'd turn the air blue if she tried to voice her thoughts; two, because she was certain she'd burst into tears if she moved so much as a muscle in her face; and three, because he was already walking away as if being near her made him sick.

But it was Jacqui who felt nauseous.

How long she stood there in the middle of the room she wasn't sure, but the voice of the teenage waitress finally pulled her from her haze of humiliation.

'What would you like for breakfast this morning, Ms Raynor?' she asked.

Jacqui laughed bitterly through a mist of burning tears. 'A lethal dose of arsenic would pick my day right up!'

The October sky was cloudless, with the sun still short of its peak when they reached the shoot-site at the creek. Unlike the previous time they'd been here, Jacqui was oblivious to the native beauty of the area. The tall gum-trees on either side of the crystal ribbon of water might have shielded them from prying eyes, but even before she climbed into the back of the Land Rover and undressed she felt cruelly exposed.

Now, sitting naked beneath a full-length towelling robe while several metres away Flanagan set up his tripod, she was fighting to keep a hold on her control. Her insides were being ripped apart by such violently strong emotions that she wasn't sure whether she wanted to scream with rage or sob with humiliation.

She could think of a dozen words she'd heard when she'd been growing up that she wanted to hurl at the man working close by, but saying them out loud seemed beyond her. Not that it mattered—calling him a heartless, hormone-driven lump of pond scum would have been too flattering!

You can't lay all the blame on him, her conscience chided. She sighed, knowing that it was the self-disgust wedged in her throat that kept her tirade of abuse a silent one. Still, it scared her that she couldn't vent her anger, couldn't rid herself of the confusion pouring through her blood and flooding her brain.

On some bizarre level she felt as if she understood how her niece, Simone, felt immediately prior to one of her infamous tantrums. But, even though her niece always slipped into an angelic state of serenity following such outbursts, Jacqui knew a similar self-purging exercise wasn't an option for her. Society was less tolerant of twenty-five-year-olds throwing themselves on the ground and kicking and screaming.

'You about ready?' he called to her.

She swallowed down her denial. He was so calm, so remotely professional that in that instant she hated him. Hadn't last night touched him at all? How was it possible that she could have lost herself so completely in their lovemaking and he could be immune to its effects—so immune that he hadn't even made a passing reference to it? Not that *she* had, but, then again, if she tasted any more humiliation today she'd need her stomach pumped!

'Hey!' he roared. 'I asked if you were ready to start! Is something bothering you, or what?'

She wished she had the nerve to say, Yeah Flanagan, how big a clue do you want? But she didn't.

'Dammit, Jacqui,' he complained, running a hand through his hair. 'Are you just going to sit there——?'

'Keep your shirt on, Flanagan!' she yelled back. 'I'm coming.' She stood up and forced her feet to move in his direction. Pride was her motivation.

She wouldn't even *think* about last night from this point onwards. She'd get through this shoot and every other one after it without once thinking of how magical his hands had felt on her body even if it killed her! The only thing she was going to remember about Flanagan's hands was that they held a camera. And with any luck she'd be so coolly professional that Patric too-sexy-for-*her*-own-good Flanagan would end up with terminal frostbite!

*   *   *

Patric again put his eye to the viewfinder and focused in on Jacqui. She was sitting with her back to the camera, in a cross-legged yoga position, with her hands resting on her knees. Her long blonde hair was pulled over one shoulder and reflected the sunlight as spectacularly as the crystal-clear water of the creek, which splashed against the rock before continuing its dance downstream.

The mix of colours in the picture would be fabulous—the intense blue of the sky above a horizon of treetop-green-covered mountains, the beige trunks of towering gumtrees stretching down to the cool, polished silver of the creek, and there, in the centre, Jacqui's golden head and creamy white skin. And...

Ah, hell! Part of her bundled-up robe was in the shot!

'Jacqui!' he shouted, standing away from the camera. 'Drop the dressing-gown; it's in the shot.' He bent back to the camera, still talking. 'We're trying to capture the rawness of nature here, not——' He jerked his head back. *This* time his view was of Jacqui awkwardly pulling the damn robe back on!

'Give me strength!' he muttered, imploring any or all higher life-forms to intercede on his behalf.

Again he moved from the camera, concentrating hard on gritting his teeth in an effort to rein in his emotions. He cursed softly as the action only made him more tense, and began kneading his neck with his left hand while rotating his right shoulder in the hope of gaining some measure of physical relief.

Would this shoot *never* end? More importantly, would they ever get it started? He watched Jacqui wade back from the centre of the creek, clutching at her robe as if hiding some hideous deformity. He knew better.

He pulled his sunglasses from their resting-place on the top of his head to dull the impact of her approach on his senses.

It was a totally futile attempt at self-defence because, unbidden, his memory detailed every inch of what lay beneath the fluffy white towelling—the soft expanse of satin-soft skin, the high, rose-tipped breasts, the flat, firm stomach that had contracted with excitement beneath his hands, and the taut buttocks above long, hard-hugging legs. The most exquisite body he'd ever seen—or known.

A shudder of desire gripped his body, bringing a groan so close to his lips that for a moment he thought it had escaped, and suddenly his neck muscles threatened to be the least of his physical problems!

Quickly he pushed the thought aside, reminding himself that this woman, who'd given herself so readily to him, was living with another man. He might have forgotten it last night in the heat of passion, but he sure wasn't going to let it happen again. No way! It was bad enough that she was screwing up his shooting schedule—there was no way he was going to let her screw up his life!

'Damnation, Jacqui!' he snapped, airing his frustration in anger. 'What's your problem *now*?' So far she'd complained that the sun was in her eyes, that the rock he wanted her to pose on was too hard, and that the water was too cold. Well, he'd had all he could take and he'd be damned if he'd fall victim to the wounded look in her eyes. 'Well, spit it out!'

Jacqui quelled the desire to cry, telling herself that no photographer had ever had the satisfaction of reducing her to tears, and that hell would freeze over before she granted it to Patric Flanagan. He might have scored a first with her body, but it ended there!

'My problem,' she said tersely, 'is that you won't let me sit on my robe, and when I hold it it's getting in the shot. I need a plastic bag.'

'A plastic bag?'

'Yes. To put——' she tugged at the garment she wore '—this in.'

'Look, Jacqui,' he said through clenched teeth. 'Put the bloody thing anywhere you like! Just get back out on that rock!'

She nodded. 'Do you have one?'

'One what?'

'Plastic bag. A big one. And some string.'

'String?' He was barely holding on to his temper.

'So I can tie the top of the bag with one end of it and tie the other on to my toe——'

'Why, in the name of all things holy, do you want to tie the thing to your foot?'

'Because otherwise the bag will float away,' she explained, watching his fingers rake through his hair and remembering how it had felt when her own had done it.

'Forget the string, the bag, and every other stupid thing going on in your head, and get out on that rock!' He held his arm towards her. 'I'll take care of your damn robe.'

'If you think I'm going to strip and walk naked out there you're——'

'It's about twelve hours too late for a pseudo-attack of modesty, don't you think?' His voice was cool and cruel. 'I've seen everything worth seeing. And, believe me, I'm not interested in another session of one-on-one lust.'

Lust. The way he said it told her that he would no doubt describe what they'd shared last night with a far more crude four-letter word.

The taste of bile seemed to start in her mouth and burn through her entire body. Jacqui had never felt so sick in her entire life. Nor so stupid. So really, really dumb! She wished instant death for herself, but no one granted it. She wished a retrospective death for Flanagan, but was equally disappointed. She wished that she could come up with a really cutting retort, but even that was hopeless.

'Jacqui?'

His voice was impatient and impersonal, yet it compelled her to move—it was either that or break down in front of him. Blinking back tears, she reached to untie the belt securing the sole article of clothing she wore, but before her fingers even began to move on the knot her wrist was caught in a hard male grip. Her breath froze in her lungs.

'Wear it out to the rock. When you're ready I'll come and get it.'

She didn't look up or respond in any way to his words until he let go of her hand. Then she turned and waded back into the calf-deep water.

The warm tears tracking down her face were in stark contrast to the coldness of the creek and the ice crusting her heart. How could she have been so stupid? Why couldn't she have kept Flanagan at arm's length as she'd done with every other man who'd tried to bed her over the years? Why couldn't fate have thrown her at one of them?

Why, when she had been able to withstand being wooed with flowers and gifts, being plied with copious quantities of champagne and charm, had she succumbed so easily to Flanagan—a man who'd only 'courted' her with arguments, aggravation and avoidance?

Oh, God, what had happened to her pride? Forget the pride, what had happened to her common sense? She had to work with this man!

How many times in her career had she sat around consoling sobbing colleagues after they'd yielded to the temptation of an affair with an associate? Dozens, she recalled ruefully. And how many times had she vowed not to make the same mistake? Plenty! Millions! Countless times! More than enough to know better.

But had she? Oh, no! The very first time that Jacqui I'd-never-put-myself-in-that-position Raynor had found herself facing the ultimate temptation, she'd tumbled into the man's arms without a second thought. Actually, she couldn't even recall if she'd had a *first* thought. One look into Flanagan's seductive brown eyes and her brain had seized!

The urge to sniff made Jacqui realise that her tears were no longer a trickle but a deluge. Darn! Things were bad when a person could cry and not know she was doing it. Thank God Flanagan was too far away to hear, or that would have been more embarrassment that she could do without, especially since she had to work with the guy until who knew when. And she was legally bound to work for him. She had no options. Well, technically she could have fought the contract, but since she had no money...

She mentally sighed. Never before had the burden of her father's debts seemed so heavy. But, she decided, instead of letting them get her down she would use them as positive motivation to get through the rest of her time with Flanagan. She remembered reading somewhere that one of the top international models had said that the only way she got through some shoots was to 'think of the big bucks at the end'.

That was what *she* would do. She'd concentrate on the fact that at the end of this assignment, or very shortly after, she'd have the cash to pay off the people that her father had unwittingly defrauded. Once that was done she wouldn't have to smile again unless she felt like it!

Even if she couldn't forget what had happened last night she would pull herself together enough so that the shoot would run smoothly and be over quickly! Once it was, Flanagan's face, like his touch, would be only a memory!

Sensing reborn strength, Jacqui mopped her face with the end of her belt, hesitating for only a second before slipping the robe from her shoulders. Then, carefully, so as not to reveal more than necessary to the man standing on shore, she wriggled free of the garment.

She braced herself for the discomfort of the rough sandstone beneath her buttocks, then gingerly edged the fabric from beneath her, not wanting to fall into the creek. While the thought of death still seemed like the least of a whole heap of evils, she didn't want to experience one where her life would supposedly flash before her eyes. The last thing she needed was a video replay of her past—especially her *recent* past.

At the sound of Flanagan's splashing approach Jacqui's traitorous heart sped up, and no amount of silent commands for it to behave made any difference.

Irritated, she rolled the robe into a tight ball and was securing the belt around it when his voice cut the silence.

'OK, give it to me.'

He sounded about a metre away, and yet her skin tingled as if he'd reached out and touched her. The recollection of exactly how gentle his touch could be sent such a hot flame of desire rocketing through her that her nipples immediately hardened.

Then, seemingly without any directive from her brain, her tongue began moving around her mouth, as if trying to detect any lingering taste of the male one which only hours before had initiated her to experiences she'd never dreamed of. Such thoughts were making her sway with sensual weakness.

'Jacqui, give me the flippin' robe, will you?'

Feeling more foolish than ever, and grateful that the length of her hair concealed her bareness, she extended her arm behind her.

'H-here.' He took so long to take it that she thought for an instant that he must have gone back, but she wasn't risking turning round to check. Concealing her face, which after her crying jag was bound to be blotchy and red, was suddenly as imperative as concealing her body from him. More so. Because it would reveal that he had the power to hurt her.

'Flanagan, take it before I get a cramp in my arm!'

She heard him swear at the same instant as she pulled back from the brush of his fingers against hers. Then all she could think about was stopping herself from falling into the water while trying to preserve her modesty at the same time. Somehow she managed it.

'Brilliant!' Flanagan exclaimed, and she knew that he wasn't talking about her balancing act. 'Look what you've done!' he said, presenting her peripheral vision with a lump of dripping wet material.

'What *I've* done!' she exploded, barely staying balanced on the awkwardly shaped rock as her brain immediately checked her body's instinct to turn to him.

'You should have waited until I had a better grip on it before you let go,' he insisted.

'You should've given me a plastic bag when I asked for it!' she countered with her back to him. 'Now what do I do?'

'What you're being paid to do! Pose!' he snapped. 'You claimed to be a model, remember?'

'I *am* a model!'

'Good, then perhaps we'll finally finish what we started nearly two hours ago!' came the response. 'We've still got another shoot to get through today.'

'Don't remind me,' she muttered over her shoulder to his departing back. 'I can only live one nightmare at a time.'

Focusing on a distant tree, Jacqui draped her hair over her left shoulder, baring herself from shoulder to buttocks and, taking a deep breath, mutinously assumed the cross-legged pose he wanted.

CHAPTER TEN

PATRIC stepped away from the camera and mopped at the perspiration coating his face. What wouldn't he give for a sudden onset of Canadian winter now? He cursed as his conscience told him that he was deluding himself if he thought that the climate was the cause of the anger and frustration knotting his gut.

The truth was that he already knew that the developed prints of what he'd shot so far this morning would stink. More annoying was having to acknowledge that even if they stayed here all day what he'd already got was as good as he was going to get.

'OK, Jacqui, that'll do!' he shouted. She gave no indication of having heard him, but then he wasn't surprised. She'd been statue-still for the last thirty minutes, even though he'd nearly sent himself hoarse telling her to relax. Corpses in the morgue would have looked more life-like than she had!

'Hoy! Jacqui!' he bellowed. 'I said that's it! You can come in now!'

Out on the rock her blonde head turned slightly. 'Bring me something to put on first!'

His initial instinct was to refuse—but, hell, he couldn't take the strain. If it had been torture focusing in on the back view of her nakedness for the last forty-five minutes, then watching her walk towards him would be hormonal suicide. Swearing under his breath, he tugged his sunglasses down on to his nose, as if they would dim the mental image of her doing just that, then snatched his shirt from the ground and waded into the water.

Jacqui frowned over her shoulder at the khaki shirt held out to her. 'My clothes are in a nylon rucksack in the front of the car.'

His sigh was heavy with martyrdom. 'Just put this on for now. It's not a damn fashion show; no one's going to see you in the few seconds it'll take you to walk——' His words ended in a succinct curse, but it wasn't what he said that caused Jacqui to blanch, it was the touch of his hand on her shoulder.

'You're burnt!' he accused. 'Didn't I tell you to put sunscreen on?'

'I did.'

'Garbage, Jacqui! Your back is pink.'

His words reminded her to toss her hair back over her shoulder to conceal the expanse of flesh she'd forgotten was displayed. As his hand reached for her chin she pulled away.

'I just want to see your face——' he started.

'My face is fine. I put sunscreen everywhere I could reach,' she told him, hurriedly slipping her arms into his shirt.

'Which might have been fine if you'd been a contortionist!' he chided. 'The last thing I need is a blistered and peeling mod——'

'I tan easily,' she said, buttoning the shirt and trying to gauge exactly how much of her it would cover before she stood up. 'It'll be gone by morning.'

'Huh!' His tone was unconvinced. 'You're lucky that this afternoon's shots are all frontals.'

Oh, yeah, she thought, lowering her feet into the water; I couldn't be more blessed!

While Patric packed up his camera gear Jacqui climbed into the Land Rover to swap the masculine shirt for a pair of bikini pants and an oversized T-shirt which reached to mid-thigh. It was no use wishing the day was over, because she still had tomorrow, and the day after, and the day after *that* and all the rest to confront. She shoved her sunglasses on and checked the side-mirror of the car—not for her own reflection, but to calculate how much breathing space she had before Flanagan hauled himself into the seat next to her.

His back was to her and he was in the process of folding up the camera tripod. He was shoeless and his jeans were rolled almost to his knees, the ends wet from his foray into the creek. His bare torso glistened in the noonday sun, and unconsciously her fingers fluttered, as if anxious to touch the sleek mahogany skin and feel the muscles move beneath it.

The memory of how they'd responded to her last night made her groan and close her eyes—touching him had been every bit as arousing as being touched by him. Well . . . almost.

The sound of him at the rear of the vehicle caused her eyes to fly open, and the discovery that she was holding his shirt to her breast and of how close she'd come to being caught doing so made her furious! She flung it on to the driver's seat and edged closer to the door.

He climbed in and started the engine with curt, angry movements before revving the engine and quickly releasing the handbrake. Jacqui was jolted against the door as he swung them into a tight turn then accelerated towards the rough bush track they'd come along earlier. While she wasn't stupid enough to think that off-road driving, even in a four-wheel drive, was supposed to be smooth, it seemed to her that Flanagan wasn't making any effort to avoid the worst sections of ground. She'd had only one filling to date, but, considering the teeth-rattling way he was negotiating the track back to the main road, there was a strong chance that she'd be wearing dentures in the not too distant future!

On cue she was bounced off the seat, and she butted her head against the roof. Grabbing the dashboard with one hand and the side of the door with the other, she swung her face to the driver. 'Hey, go easy, will you! This crate is going to fall apart!' They became almost airborne and she gasped.

'Listen,' he said through gritted teeth. 'Quit complaining, OK? I've had a gutful of it from you today!'

If she hadn't had to hold on for grim life Jacqui would have punched him. *He'd* had a gutful? He'd done nothing but roar at her the whole time she'd been posing for him!

'Your shoulders are too tense; relax...! You're slouching! Straighten your back! Get that flyaway strand of hair out of the way! Relax! Dammit, Jacqui, I thought you said you were a professional? *Loosen up*!'

If she'd had the money she'd have put a contract out on his life! If she'd had a gun she'd have shot him herself—and not just for the personal satisfaction! Compared to this a gaol term would have seemed like a holiday in paradise!

She looked down at the slogan on the T-shirt she wore—Life's a bitch and then...you die! Only on a good day, she thought. Only on a *good* day!

Patric watched her trying to unseal the sandwiches the hotel had packed, tormenting himself with the thought that last night those unpolished but perfectly manicured nails had been scraping his skin and not plastic wrap. And he was subjected to even more pain as the same long, slim fingers lifted ham-filled bread to perfectly formed lips and even white teeth, which opened and then closed around it.

Arousal rippled through his blood and he looked at his left shoulder, expecting to see traces of the perfect indentation he'd worn on waking. The delicate bite-mark was gone, so his eyes reverted to the source of his awareness.

She sat in the shade of a huge gum-tree only a few feet from him. Her hair billowed down over her shoulders and her long legs were stretched elegantly out in front of her.

If it hadn't been for the succulent way her navy T-shirt hugged the curves of her body, she'd have passed for a fourteen-year-old. Yet, for all the youthful innocence she personified, sitting there sipping a can of cola, Flanagan's body was still reacting to the wanton sensuality she'd exhibited last night.

He wondered if she could feel the heated desire radiating in him, if her loins were also melting from it. He groaned. Apparently aloud.

'What's up?' she asked, her voice neutral.

He almost laughed at the irony of her question. If he told her, what reaction would he get? She was gazing right at him, but though she'd discarded her sunglasses her eyes were shaded by the peak of her baseball cap and impossible to read.

'Nothing.' He grabbed a cold drink from the small coolbag they'd brought and opened it. After a long swallow that emptied half the can he clamped its coolness in his lap, where it would do the most good, and picked up a sandwich to feed the one appetite he didn't have!

Twenty minutes later, with lunch packed away, it was time to explain what he wanted Jacqui to do. The idea was for her to stroll slowly down the slope of the hill situated to their west, with her hand extended and trailing over the waist-high grass. Ideally he'd have liked a light breeze to be lifting her hair out so that in the finished photograph it would look like strands of gold spread against the vivid cloudless sky, but there was never a breeze when you needed one.

'So do you understand what I'm aiming for?' he asked her.

'I think so,' she said, stretching her arms behind her neck to lift her hair away from her neck.

The action made Patric swallow hard—the way her T-shirt pulled tight against her obviously braless breasts made *him* hard. Willing his thoughts to anything other than the woman in front of him, he tried to concentrate on the normally simple task of putting a fresh roll of film into his camera.

Jacqui was hit by a fresh onslaught of nerves as she watched Flanagan load the camera and then point it in the direction of where she was to pose. This was going to be much worse than last time, because this time she would have to *face* him in her nakedness. It didn't matter that they'd be separated by roughly three hundred metres, because the powerful camera would allow him to see her face as clearly as if she was standing in front of him.

'How far do I have to go?' she asked. When the bent dark head ignored her she repeated the question.

'Huh? Pardon?' Flanagan's totally distracted expression infuriated her.

'I asked how far up the hill do you want me to go?'

'About three-quarters of the way. A wide-angle lens will ensure I get in everything.'

Wouldn't it though, she thought as she turned away.

'Hey, and do a bit better than you did last time, huh?'

The words stopped her in her tracks and she swung around to glare at him.

'What's that supposed to mean?' she challenged.

'That I want you relaxed. I want a dreamy look on your face. A real nature's child type of thing—understand? I don't want you looking like a store mannequin that's been stuck in a paddock this time instead of on a rock,' he said drily.

Jacqui's blood boiled and she jutted her chin at the unfair criticism.

'Listen,' she said, with sheathed aggression, 'I have a reputation in the modelling business for being able to deliver exactly what a photographer wants.'

'Is that so?'

'Yes!' She defiantly flicked her hair over her shoulder. 'I gave you exactly what you asked for,' she continued. 'If you are unhappy with the results then it'll be because you weren't specific enough with the directions, Flanagan!'

A wry grin tugged at his mouth. 'So you're saying I wasn't explicit enough?'

'Bingo!' she said. 'I can hardly be expected to read minds—especially where one doesn't exist!'

He grabbed her arm and hauled her up against him. 'If my mind has become non-existent it's entirely your fault.'

'Let me go!'

'Uh-uh,' he murmured, moving one hand to her bottom and drawing her lower body up against his own. 'Not until I show you just how explicit I can be. Oh, and forget the mind-reading, babe,' he advised, lowering his head. 'Concentrate on the body language.'

The feel of his mouth against her own stunned her, not because she'd not known the kiss was coming, but because it was so ruthlessly cold compared to those he'd lavished her with the night before. Insulting was the only word to describe it, but to her surprise she was released even before she had a chance to struggle.

'Ah, hell!' he said, running both hands through his hair.

'Don't you *ever* do that again!' she screamed, jumping away when he stretched a tentative hand in her direction.

Her reaction made Patric feel like the lowest form of life. What the hell had he been trying to prove? And to whom?

'Jacqui, I'm sorry.'

'Good, then it's unanimous!' she said, giving him a lethal stare.

He shoved his hands in his pockets and took a steadying breath. 'We need to talk about last night,' he said, meeting her gaze squarely. 'Clear things up between us.'

'The only thing I want clear, Flanagan, is that it won't happen again. I'm not a tramp! Contrary to what you may think after last night, I'm not in the habit of whoring around!'

Bending down, she picked up the bag which held sunblock, a hair brush and would shortly contain the clothes she now wore, and began to walk away. 'Let's get this over and done with a.s.a.p., Flanagan.'

He hesitated for a moment, then called her name.

'Now what?' she snapped, spinning to face him.

'Just for the record, I don't think you're a tramp,' he said softly.

She gave a bitter laugh. 'Well, I sure as hell feel like one!'

CHAPTER ELEVEN

THE heat was so punishing that Jacqui decided the sun was shining straight from hell. She coated her bare flesh with yet another layer of sunscreen and waited for the signal from Flanagan telling her to start her descent down the slope.

She was standing in almost bust-height grass and, despite the way it prickled her skin, wished it several centimetres higher. At least it would've covered two more of her femininely vital parts. Still, at least she could get away with keeping her knickers and trainers on this time. As for future shoots...well, she feared the worst was yet to come!

In an effort to get some relief from the heat, she lifted the hair from her neck. While she acknowledged that, topless, the action was provocative in the extreme, she also knew that distance kept her safe from the eyes of the man below.

So far Flanagan hadn't approached the camera, and that meant that to his naked eye she'd appear as he did to her—little more than an indistinct figure. Of course, that would all change the moment he stepped up to the tripod and waved his shirt.

'*Then* kiddo,' she told herself, 'you start thinking of the money!'

The scream literally curdled Patric's blood, and instinctively he looked to the spot where Jacqui had been standing. Now she was some distance below it, and racing down the hill as if the devil himself was after her.

Leaping from his haunches, he sprinted across the uneven ground, closing the gap between them while simultaneously visually scouting to see who or what had startled her. When he was within twelve feet of her she all but flew into his arms, nearly knocking the breath out of him.

'God, Jacqui! What's happened?'

'He w-w-was staring at...at me! L-l-looking like he was g-g-going...' Her rapid speech was made more incoherent by breathlessness and the way her body quaked.

'Hush, hush. Honey, it's OK. You're OK. I'm here.' He held her tightly against him, one hand wrapped around her lightly oiled body and the other stroking her hair.

'Oh...God...h-h-he was w-w-watching me!' Her fingers clutched partly at his open shirt and partly at his haired chest as she continued shaking and stammering. 'All that t-t-time he was s-sitting there w-w-watch——'

'You're safe now, honey. It's all right now.' As he spoke Patric continued to eye the hillside, trying to find the man who'd reduced one of the toughest women he'd ever met to a sobbing, terrified wreck. He'd break the perverted bastard's neck, and smile doing it!

For an instant he thought he was being given the chance as the grass began to sway, but his hopes were dashed by the realisation that the front end of a southerly had arrived, and it was only the wind sweeping the grass and making it dance.

Another shiver came from the woman in his arms and he squeezed her even closer. 'Steady, sweetheart. I've got you now.'

'His—face...' Again she shuddered. 'Ugh! He was...was so ug-ugly. And...and...'

'Easy, babe,' he whispered, gently running his hand up and down her back. 'It's OK. He didn't get you.' He felt her nod against his chest. 'Attagirl. Settle down, you're safe now.'

Once more his eyes scouted the area where she'd been. The son of a bitch was probably hiding. He continued to croon gentle reassurances, and after a few minutes he felt her still against him as the tension drained from her body.

'Feeling better?' he asked, and received a muffled affirmative response. 'Want to tell me what he looked like?' Patric raised the idea almost absently as he focused on the landscape—not merely because he wanted to catch sight of the creep who'd frightened her, but also because he was beginning to need a distraction from the warm female curves nestling softly against him.

'Ugly!' she said with feeling. 'Ugly and...*evil*. His eyes were like...like glass.' Jacqui couldn't help the tremor that went through her at the memory. Instinctively she pressed herself closer to her rescuer. It didn't matter that she didn't actually *like* Flanagan—she trusted him. Trusted him to keep her safe, to protect her.

It wasn't until her fingers were being prised from the front of his shirt that her mind was able to look beyond the horror of the hill. It dawned on her that Flanagan, though still holding her, was trying to shrug out of his shirt. A new wave of panic flooded her system at the thought of her nakedness merging with his.

'Relax,' she was told. 'I'm going to slip my shirt over your shoulders and turn around while you put it on. OK?'

Her sigh of relief and the movement of her arms to shield her breasts summoned a dry male chuckle.

'Thought you'd jumped from the frying-pan into the fire, huh?'

'N-no,' she said as he stepped back and turned away from her. 'Not exactly.' She quickly slid her arms into the shirt and began buttoning it. Even now her fingers were less than steady.

'Decent yet?'

She nodded before realising that while his broad muscular back was far superior to any other man's it still didn't have eyes. 'I... You can t-turn around,' she stammered.

For the first time she raised her face to him, and wasn't surprised to see a frown crease his brow.

'I know,' she said, striving for lightness. 'The red blotchy look doesn't work for me.'

He smiled and let his gaze skim to her bare legs. 'My shirt sure does.'

If his words did nothing else at least they evened out the colour in her face as she blushed from the neck up.

'C'mon, Jacqui,' he said, putting an arm across her shoulders. 'Let's call it a day.'

She nodded, content to forget *all* of her life beyond that moment.

'We'll contact the police as soon as we get back into town.'

His words froze her steps. 'The police?'

'We have to report this.'

'We do?'

His smile was sympathetic. 'You know we do. You can't just ignore something like this.'

'Why not?'

'Because this type of thing has to be investigated. Look, it won't be that bad,' he assured her. 'I'll be with you.'

He was probably right, she conceded. What did *she* know about how things were done in the country? She just hoped that the police wouldn't want to know what she'd been wearing at the time.

While Flanagan packed up his gear she changed into the shorts and shirt she'd worn when she'd left the hotel that morning. Then, sipping on a much needed can of soft drink, she kept herself busy trying to think of the last time she'd had such a diabolical twenty-four hours. Nothing came to mind.

When Flanagan finally eased himself behind the steering wheel he was frowning.

'What about the bag you had?' He nodded towards where she'd posed earlier and, following his gaze, she couldn't repress a shiver of distaste.

'I left it there. I couldn't think of anything except getting away.'

'You want me to go and get——?'

'No!' The thought of it terrified her. 'He could still be up there; he could——'

He grasped her hand. 'OK, OK. I won't go.'

She sank back in her seat, breathing more easily.

'Besides,' he said, gunning the engine, 'at least it'll show the cops the exact spot where it happened.' He darted her a quick look. 'About how far away from you was he?'

Again a shiver skipped down her spine. 'A . . . a metre, I'd say, tops.'

The thought of the bastard being that close to her turned Patric's blood instantly cold.

'Are you sure this is necessary?' Jacqui asked as they approached the front desk of the small country police station.

'Yes.'

'G'day.' A huge, blue-uniformed officer wearing sergeant stripes moved to the desk. 'Sergeant Taylor. How can I help you folks?'

'We'd like to report a pervert——'

'A what?' the sergeant and Jacqui said in unison.

'A pervert,' Patric repeated.

'I'll be damned,' Taylor said, then chuckled. 'This'll perk the boys up. Can't say we've had one of them round here before.'

Patric, seeing Jacqui's confused wide-eyed gaze, knew that she wasn't up to dealing with an insensitive, over-weight, underworked country cop, and decided to save her the hassle of correcting him.

'Well, you do now, Sergeant,' he said. 'He caused this woman a great deal of distress only an hour ago, and I hate to think what would have happened if she'd been alone.'

'Quite so. Well, I'll need to get a description from both of you and——'

'I didn't actually see him,' Patric explained. 'I was some distance away and came running when I heard Jacqui—Ms Raynor—scream. I——'

He stopped as his recalling the incident caused Jacqui to lay her face and arms on the counter sobbing.

'Ah, hell, honey,' he said, immediately laying his hands on her shaking shoulders. 'It's all ov——'

Sergeant Taylor bellowed for someone to bring a cup of tea with plenty of sugar. 'It's shock, of course,' he told Patric. 'Here, let me talk to her. Miss? Miss?'

Jacqui raised her face a fraction and found herself looking into the blurred image of the sergeant, who'd squatted down until his three chins were resting on the opposite side of the counter to hers. She wiped the tears from her eyes, but it was no use—the moment the man opened his mouth they started all over again.

'Now, now. I know these sickos can seem pretty threatening, but statistics show that they rarely actually carry out their threats. You'll probably be safe——'

'Oh, great job, Sergeant! That's hardly what I'd call reassuring her!' Flanagan's voice was swimming with irritation, but the policeman paid him no heed and continued to address her.

'Did you get a good look at him?'

She nodded.

'Great, great. That'll be a big help. Now, what did the mongrel look like?'

'He...he...' Trying to speak was almost beyond her. 'He was...a *snake*!'

'Yes, well, I'd use stronger words. But what I really need from you is a more accurate description. How old was he?'

Unable to speak, Jacqui backed away from the counter, shaking her head as a raucous burst of laughter burst from her.

'Oh, cripes,' muttered the sergeant. 'She's hysterical.'

In that instant she saw a glimmer of understanding dart across Flanagan's face, but the desk sergeant still looked worried.

'You...don't...don't understand,' she stuttered between giggles. 'He *was* a...a snake! A...real live... h-hissing snake!'

'Is this some kind of joke?' Sergeant Taylor demanded to know.

A wide grin broke on Flanagan's face. 'I didn't think so at first,' he said, trying to contain his amusement long enough to placate the now angry-looking policeman. 'But, you gotta admit, it's bloody funny!'

He was still smiling as Jacqui carried two glasses of beer and a bag of peanuts from the bar and deposited them on the table. She'd insisted on buying the drinks, saying that it was her way of repaying him for saving her life. Personally, Patric could have suggested and would have preferred something a lot different!

After sitting down opposite him she grinned, lifting her glass in a toast. 'To me—for saving us from being charged with filing a mischievous complaint.'

Patric pulled his glass back before it clinked with hers. 'In a pig's eye!'

'Uh-uh, Flanagan. I don't think you should make threats towards nice Sergeant Taylor,' she chided.

'Very funny!'

'I'll say!' She laughed. 'Oh, Lord, Flanagan! I can't believe you tried to have a snake arrested!'

'Me? You went along with it——'

'Only reluctantly,' she reminded him, tearing open the bag of peanuts and placing them in the centre of the table. 'I did point out that I thought it unnecessary, but——' she shrugged '—when you insisted...'

'Well, if you'd *said* it was a goddamn snake in the first place,' he said, 'or at *any* point, I wouldn't have.'

'I thought you'd realised. I mean it's not like I was shouting, Help—pervert! at the top of my lungs.'

'You weren't shouting, Help—snake! either,' he pointed out. 'Besides, your reaction was way over the top for something as mundane as a snake.'

'Mundane? It was a *black* snake! Those little cuties can kill you like——' she snapped her fingers '—that.'

'OK, but what about the sex?'

Jacqui nearly choked on her beer.

'You kept saying *he*. If you'd said *it* I'd have picked up right off what you were gibbering about.'

'I guess I just associate all snakes with being male,' she said, relieved that he was talking about the serpent's sex and nothing more personal. 'Or——' she grinned '—do I mean that the other way round—that I associate all males with being snakes?'

'Do you?' he countered, his brown eyes serious as they held hers.

She held his gaze. 'Not all.'

'But most.'

'A few. So tell me,' she said, quickly searching her brain for a safe change of topic, 'er—what's going to happen now that a reptile has ruined your plans of getting that grassy slope shot?'

He raised a speculative eyebrow. 'Has it?'

'There is *no way*, Flanagan,' she said, 'that you are going to get me back up there in this decade!'

'The snake will have moved by tomorrow,' he said.

'I don't care if the stupid thing is at this moment emigrating to Ireland; I'm not going up there again!'

'What about your bag?'

'Let the snake have it!' His half-smile was so gorgeous that she immediately wanted to provoke it further. 'Who knows?' she went on. 'Nylon rucksacks are probably as big a fashion statement in the reptile world as snakeskin ones are in ours.'

His genuine amusement somehow intensified her own, but the lightness of their shared laughter quickly thickened into a silent, electric exchange of glances.

The thickly lashed brown eyes of the man opposite held her mesmerised, and because of the sensual heat they created within her it took Jacqui a long time to separate the two messages flashing in their depths. Finally she did. One was a whispered promise of short-term physical pleasure beyond anything she'd ever known, and the other was a shouted warning against long-term emotional expectations.

Yet surely, her own eyes queried, an enormous short-term profit offset the long-term loss? But, before she could read an answer in the deep brown eyes opposite, thick lashes closed over them.

Jacqui, still wavering on the fringes of the trance, was only dimly aware of Flanagan reaching for his glass. Yet the instant he raised it to his lips—lips that in the last twenty-four hours had both worshipped and insulted her own—and began drinking, her concentration was immediately drawn to the long column of his tanned masculine throat.

It seemed as if an invisible thread linked the muscles in his neck to those in her lower abdomen, and that with each swallow he took the movement of his Adam's apple tugged that thread tighter and tighter. When he lowered the glass and used the tip of his tongue to capture the trace of froth clinging to his lip, the strength in Jacqui's hands dissolved to a point where the peanuts she'd been holding fell to the table.

'Whoa.' Flanagan reached over to slow her hasty efforts to pick up the nuts. 'You're still pretty shaken up about what happened, aren't you?'

She knew that his smile was intended to be comforting, to calm her, but unfortunately it was negated by the effect of his thumb stroking her hand. Her insides were sparking as if someone was trying to weld her ribs together! And she was grateful that Flanagan had interpreted her clumsiness as stemming from fraught nerves rather than fraught hormones.

She snatched her hand away. 'Considering it's my first encounter of the reptilian kind, that's to be expected, wouldn't you say?'

'Sure,' Patric responded, suspecting that *something* had to be responsible for the way she'd gone from laughingly relaxed to aggressively tense.

'So, Flanagan,' she continued, 'you either do without the shots you wanted on the hill——' her tone was all business '—or you do them with another model.'

Considering how moody she is right now, Patric mused, now isn't going to be a real good time to tell her

that I got a full roll of candid shots of her with my hand-
held! No, discretion was def——

His thoughts were cut short by the arrival of the sour-
faced manageress at the table.

'Ms Raynor,' she said, 'there's a man called Phil Mich-
something on the phone. He says it's——'

Jacqui leapt from her chair and grabbed the woman's
arm. 'What phone? Where? In the bar?'

'In Recep——' The woman's reply was cut short in
the wake of the mini-cyclone which blew up as Jacqui
sped from the room.

'Must be someone really important,' the manageress
mused aloud.

'Yeah.' Patric tossed back the rest of his beer. 'Sure
looks that way.'

He was midway through his second beer when an
excited-looking Jacqui all but ran to his table.

'I'm going back to Sydney.'

'*What*?'

'Only for a week or so,' she went on, as if he hadn't
spoken. 'Ten days tops.'

'No way!' he said. 'We're already behind
schedule——'

'I know, but I have to go——'

'No!' He thumped the table, toppling both glasses;
the action clearly surprised her, but he was too enraged
to care about the spilt drinks. 'You agreed to this trip
knowing it would take three weeks when we left Sydney.
If it clashed with other arrangements you should have
said so then.'

'But... I wasn't expecting this——'

'Listen, Michelini might be used to saying ''Jump''
and having you ask ''How high?'' when you're already
off the ground, but I'll be damned if I'm going to be so
quick to accommodate his whims *or* yours!'

'Listen, Flanagan, no one—least of all *me*—would call
you accommodating!' she blazed. 'And I'd tell you why,
except that firstly I'm booked on a flight which leaves

Port Macquarie in a little over an hour, and secondly the human life-span isn't that long!'

'This might be your idea of professionalism, but it sure as hell isn't mine! We've got a contract——'

'So sue me!' she challenged. 'Because the day my career becomes more important than my sister is the day——'

'What the hell has your sister got to do with it?'

'Everything! She's *pregnant*!'

'So?'

'So she's gone into premature labour!'

'Then why didn't you say so?'

'Because, Flanagan, you never gave me a chance!'

He watched her stride from the room and felt like an absolute heel—as if she hadn't had a rough enough day already, without him jumping down her throat. He sighed, knowing that the knot of jealousy which had formed in his gut the minute she'd dashed to take the phone call hadn't loosened any. Regardless of *why* she was going to Sydney, the fact remained that Michelini was still going to be there.

On that cheering thought he left the bar. The least he could do was offer to drive her to the airport. And—who knew?—with any luck he might be back on an even keel by the time she returned. No! He *would* be back on an even keel when she got back. And it was his own common sense, not luck, which would guarantee it!

The trip to Port Macquarie airport had been tense and silent. Jacqui was feeling utterly drained from the almost bizarre physical and emotional buffeting she'd taken since getting out of bed yesterday morning.

On reflection she backdated the start of her problems to the ill-fated night she'd met Flanagan for dinner. She'd been vitally aware of him ever since. But then, that was *his* fault—no man had the right to look as good as he did! Even the woman at the airline office where they'd picked up her ticket ten minutes ago had drooled over him!

Now, as she waited for the instruction to board, she smiled at the remembered incident...

While she'd had been frantically shifting her weight from one foot to the other, worrying that she'd miss the check-in deadline, the woman who had been supposed to issue her ticket had been more interested in mooning over the silently waiting Flanagan!

The immaculately groomed redhead had ignored all of Jacqui's discreet efforts to regain her attention, and had seemed blissfully ignorant of the fact that passengers were expected to check in thirty minutes before departure and it was still a five-minute drive to the terminal building. To make matters worse, when Jacqui had turned around to tell Flanagan to wait outside or she'd *never* get her ticket he'd had to go and return the woman's doe-eyed admiration with a smile! For Jacqui's patience that had been the last straw!

'Forget it,' she'd advised the woman in a sympathetic tone. 'He's gay.' At the startled disbelief directed at her she hadn't been able to resist adding, with a solemn nod, 'Camp as a row of tents.'

With a last rueful glance at Flanagan the woman had returned her attention to Jacqui. 'What a *waste*...'

Jacqui struggled to contain a grin, imagining how Flanagan, now standing beside her, would react if he knew of her fib. Her furtive sideways glance at him only reinforced her impression of his rugged masculinity, and she marvelled that the redhead hadn't laughed in her face! Ha, she thought, and they say we blondes are dumb!

She couldn't work out why Flanagan had found it necessary to wait with her until boarding-time, especially since he hadn't spoken a word. But then, nor had she encouraged conversation, since with them it invariably led to confrontation, and she wasn't up to another public slanging match. The one in the bar had been enough—not that it had been loud, but Flanagan's table-thumping had drawn one or two curious glances.

The grim line of his mouth and his crossed-arm stance told her that he was still put out about this latest disruption to his precious schedule, but Jacqui had appreciated his offer to drive her here, and was compelled to tell him so.

'No sweat,' he grunted.

'I should be back in a week.' She scribbled down the phone number of the main house. 'You can contact me on this number.' She paused, then added, 'If you need to,' not wanting to appear as if she expected it. Which she didn't.

'OK. Give me a call and let me know how things go.'

The request surprised her. 'Oh, OK.'

'And let me know when you're coming back,' he said.

'You don't have to pick me up; I can get a cab.'

'I know. I need to try and reschedule the shoot.'

'Oh, right... of course.' She felt like an absolute fool for having jumped to stupid conclusions and having been put in her place so effectively. 'Well, I guess I better go.'

'Yeah. Is someone meeting you at the airport?'

'Providing there're no hitches, hopefully Phil.'

'Right. Well, you'd best go then, huh?'

CHAPTER TWELVE

JACQUI stared out at the cotton-wool clouds enveloping the plane, and watched them merge into the even, sculptured features of Patric Flanagan. She wondered if he'd received the message she'd left with the hotel manageress that she was arriving back today—three days early. The anticipation of seeing him again was both exhilarating and scary.

Leaning her head back against the seat, she tried for the hundredth time to convince herself that she wasn't in love with him.

Give it up, Raynomovski! her mind said. You've fallen harder and faster for the guy than a brick would out of this plane!

She sighed ruefully, knowing that lying to herself was as hopeless as the entire sorry situation. Millions of guys in the world, and she had had to pick Flanagan—who not only considered models in general as being morally corrupt but Jacqui Raynor as the prime example of that corruption!

Terrific! She wasn't sure when precisely he had won her stupid, traitorous heart, but she was certain that in life's raffle of love he'd be the last person wanting to hold the winning ticket if *she* were the prize!

Her first instinct had been to stay in Sydney for as long as possible in the hope that her feelings would change. And yet, even with all the distractions that two noisy toddlers, a howling newborn and a set of bemused parents could create, Patric had stubbornly remained foremost in her mind.

So yesterday she'd decided to move to Plan C—confront the cause of her bout of lovesickness and prove that he was no longer a threat to her. After all, when

she'd had her vaccine against typhoid a few years ago
she'd initially suffered a mild fever, but after that she'd
been immune. It would be the same with Flanagan, since,
like the fever, he caused her to sleep fitfully and wake
up in a lather of sweat.

He was the first thing that Jacqui saw as she entered the
small airport lounge, and the sight of him froze her to
the spot. In that split-second she became oblivious to
everyone and everything around her save the dark-haired
man propped negligently beside the exit.

His long, denim-clad legs were crossed at the ankle
and his arms were folded across his tanned, muscular
torso. The stance was totally male and, given the fact
that he was wearing a loose-fitting black T-shirt with its
armholes slashed almost to the waist, blatantly sexy.

It took the weight of another passenger's luggage
swinging into the back of her knees to project her
forward again. Afraid of what her eyes would betray,
she lifted her sunglasses from where they hung around
her neck and shoved them on as she shortened the distance between herself and the man who seemed to have
bought time-share in her head.

'Hi, Flanagan. What are you doing here?'

'Nothing special; I often spend my Mondays hanging
out at small country airports.'

Jacqui knew that as opening lines went hers had been
pretty clichéd and had deserved his dry response. But,
since *clear* thoughts—much less original ones—would
have been a miracle given the flustered state of her brain
right now, she followed his lead.

'Really? Well, since you're here, is there any chance
I could get a lift with you?'

He frowned, as if having to give consideration to his
answer.

'Sure. Why not? I've been here for nearly forty
minutes anyway,' he said, pushing away from the wall
to tower over her.

Overawed by his sudden closeness, she tried to rally her defences. 'I didn't ask you to meet me, Flanagan.'

'I know. Give me your bag.'

The touch of his hand against hers sent an electric current straight up her arm and, seemingly without any signal from her brain, her hand released its grip on her bag.

'This all you got?'

For some reason that seemed like the hardest question she'd ever been asked, and it took her a full ten seconds to analyse it and another ten to manage an affirmative nod.

'OK, then.' He gave a lazy smile. 'Let's get out of here.'

With the effects of that smile drugging her body, Jacqui followed him in a state of slow-moving panic. This *wasn't* going to go away! This wasn't anything as innocuous as a mild case of typhoid—not by a long shot! This was something that *had* to be resolved.

These thoughts ricocheted about in her head as they walked in silence to where the Land Rover was parked.

Strangely it was the sight of the battered vehicle which jolted her to the realisation that the only reason she was here, being met by Flanagan, was that they had a business arrangement. Nothing more, nothing less. Sure, they'd slept together, but it had simply *happened*. Suddenly— without warning, without planning, without...anything!

There had never been *anything* between her and Flanagan other than a business arrangement. There still wasn't. So how could she resolve something she didn't understand? How could she rid herself of a feeling which she had no logical reason for having?

A person didn't fall in love with someone for no good reason. Yet, when she stopped to try and think of what Flanagan had done to warrant her being cursed with the sensation that the world was a whole lot better when he was with her, she came up empty!

OK, so there had been a strong physical attraction between them from the start, but Jacqui knew at least a dozen people who'd survived purely physical relationships without falling in love or becoming candidates for the funny farm. *She*, however, had not only fallen victim to warped-minded Cupid, but was rapidly approaching the stage when, if the guys in the white coats didn't come and get her soon, she was going to turn herself in voluntarily.

'You're unusually quiet. What's up?'

It was the caring tone in Flanagan's voice that caught her attention rather than his words.

'What?' she asked.

'You haven't said a word since we left the airport. What's on your mind?'

You, she replied mentally, but, instead of answering, climbed into the passenger seat and buckled her seatbelt, hoping that he'd let the question drop. No such luck! He remained standing beside her seat, making closing the door impossible, and wearing an expectant expression—an incredibly handsome expectant expression.

'Well?' he prodded when she stayed mute. 'What's up?'

'N-nothing.' She was almost drowning in his eyes; he had the most marvellous brown eyes and——

'Jacqui?'

'What makes you think something's up?'

He shrugged. 'You're quiet. You're defensive. You——'

'I'm *often* quiet, Flanagan!'

'And you're *very* often defensive,' he said quickly, then grinned. 'But usually it's because of something I've done or said, and as I've been on my best behaviour since you got off the plane I figure there must be another reason.'

'There isn't.'

'No problems in Sydney?' He looked genuinely concerned.

'Do you mean besides a severe case of sibling rivalry on the part of my niece and nephew towards their new brother, a four-day-old who won't sleep, and two sleep-deprived parents?'

His grin slammed her heart into her ribs. 'Yeah, I mean besides that.'

'Then, no. Everything at home is fine.' She shrugged. 'At least it was when I left.'

'So the only reason you're back early is because you missed me, huh?'

Jacqui gasped so hard that she almost choked, but she managed a denial none the less. 'In your dreams, Flanagan.'

Laughing, he slammed the door and walked around the front of the car. His patient good humour was both irritating and confusing—but then irritation and confusion were par for the course when Flanagan was around. Of course, recently a whole new set of emotions had come into play where he was concerned.

Dammit, Flanagan was the last person she wanted to be vulnerable to! Although *being* vulnerable to him was infinitely better than having him *know* that she was vulnerable to him! Therefore it bothered her that he was so attuned to her inner disquiet—actually, unnerved was a more apt description of how his sudden intuitiveness made her feel.

Worried that he might start drawing far more accurate conclusions if she remained untalkative, she launched into speech the instant he engaged the engine.

'So, have you done much photography since I've been gone?'

'Nope.'

When he didn't expand she fired off another safe question. 'How come? Has it been raining up here?'

'No.'

'I thought there were several local beauty spots you wanted to do without me?'

'Changed my mind.'

'Why?'

He shrugged.

Gee, she thought, pulling teeth from a rabid Rottweiler would be easier than this! She'd have got a better conversation from a store-window mannequin.

Tenaciously she tried again. 'No problems with Sergeant Taylor over the snake thing?'

'Nope.' The grin accompanying his reply made her suspect that he was aware that she was grasping at straws now, but too bad! Her pride was at stake here.

'Oh . . . well, that's good. I was worried,' she lied in a mutter, her mind racing to find something else to say.

'I was surprised to see you at the airport,' she continued, despite his look which said that she was stating the obvious. 'When I phoned from Sydney the hotel said you were out. How did you know what flight I was on? I didn't leave a message.'

She saw his smug smile side-on. 'Simple. I called and checked.'

Idiot! she chided herself. Keep this up and you'll be declared brain-dead! As furious with him as she was with herself, she grabbed the first cassette her fingers touched on and shoved it into the tape deck.

Seconds later the voice of John Cougar Mellencamp singing the raunchy, provocative 'Hurt So Good' was blaring from the speakers, and Jacqui was ready to tear her hair out!

They'd been stationary almost a minute before it registered with her that they'd stopped in the car park of one of the best hotels in Port Macquarie.

'What are we doing here?' she asked.

'This is where we're staying now. Our next three locations are between here and Coffs Harbour,' he said.

'But . . . what about my other bags? I left two suitcases at the pub.'

'Relax,' he said, jerking his thumb towards the back of the car. 'I had the manageress check your room.'

'Oh. Well . . . thanks. I'm surprised you remembered them.'

He laughed. 'Pretty hard to forget carrying anything *that* heavy.'

She pulled a face. 'How long are we here for?'

He looked at her for a moment, with a half-smile lurking at his mouth, before winking and letting it become a full-blown grin which ignited sparks in her belly. She squirmed, remembering how less than a week ago he'd fanned those sparks into a raging blaze, then single-handedly tamed them in the most——

'Er—Jacqui——' his voice from the back of the car startled her '—any reason why you're sitting in the car looking all hot and bothered when you could be inside in air-conditioned comfort having a drink?'

She blinked, only now becoming aware that she was still strapped in the passenger seat. Oh, this was ridiculous! She could hardly believe that he was affecting her so much. She quickly got out of the car.

'I don't know about you,' Flanagan said as he lifted the last of the luggage from the Land Rover, 'but right now an ice-cold beer sounds better than sex. How about it?'

Jacqui reeled at his words, her body temperature rocketing up another thousand degrees.

'Good idea,' she croaked. 'I could use a beer!' His arm brushed hers and sent a million volts of sexual electricity rushing through her body.

She leapt away, yelling, 'And—and a *shower*! Boy, I could really use a shower,' she reiterated, snatching up the nearest of her bags and hurrying towards the main entrance, desperate to put some distance between them. 'I'll—er—go and check in right now! And...have a shower. I...I'll send someone to help you with the rest of the bags,' she promised.

She ignored his amusement. Ignoring him was the only way she could hope to get both her body and mind functioning with some degree of normality. Of course, it would be easier said than done!

Jacqui's room this time was as far removed from the last one that Flanagan had booked as one could get. Not only did it run to a bedside telephone, but it had a separate lounge-dining area, and a full-size bathroom, complete with spa.

Deciding that a spa was exactly what she needed, she dumped her bag at the foot of the bed and went to turn it on. Returning to the bedroom, and knowing that she'd have to wait until the hotel staff brought the rest of her luggage, she reached for the mini-bar menu.

'Typical,' she muttered as she glanced at the prices. Why was it that things readily available in any supermarket or milk bar invariably cost three times as much in places like this? Shaking her head, she reached for an extravagantly expensive ginger ale.

A noise outside her door announced the arrival of her luggage. She was moving to open it when it swung inwards of its own accord to admit Flanagan and a teenage boy wearing a staff uniform; both were laden down with bags and camera equipment.

'Just put it down anywhere,' Flanagan told the kid. 'We'll sort it out later.'

Confused as to why he didn't have his equipment taken directly to his room, Jacqui watched mutely as he generously tipped the boy and closed the door behind him.

'What's that noise?' he asked, brushing his hair back from his forehead.

'I'm running a spa-bath.'

'Better turn it off,' he told her, with a glance that raked over her body and left it hot. 'We have to talk.'

'*Now*, Flanagan? Can't it wait? I'm——'

'Nope, it can't wait,' he cut in, taking a step towards her. '*I* can't wait.'

'Too bad,' she responded weakly as her legs timidly moved backwards to negate his determined advance. 'Because I want a...' Words failed her as her eyes became drawn to the tanned muscles which bulged in his arms as he shoved his hands into the pockets of his jeans. Oh, Lord, his body was gorgeous!

'Want what, Jacqui?' he prodded, still stalking her.

She blinked, trying to remember what—besides him— she *did* want. Oh, wonderful! On top of everything else she was having a mental breakdown. Nervously her eyes darted left, and the sight of the elegantly appointed

bathroom and rapidly filling tub cleared her foggy mind.
'A...a bath!' she exclaimed, hurrying to turn off the
tap. 'A spa to be exact.'

'Sounds good,' he said from the doorway.

'Then why don't you have one too?'

'Sounds even better.' His T-shirt was immediately
tugged over his head and dropped on to the tiled floor.

Jacqui gasped, as much in awe at the sight of his naked
male torso as from the clumsy way she'd phrased her
words. 'I meant in your own room!'

He shook his head and moved nearer. Jacqui told
herself that the only reason she didn't move away was
that the shower-screen was at her back and impeding her
retreat. Actually, it was the only thing keeping her upright, since her legs had assumed the consistency of jelly.

'Flanagan.' His name was a gasp as she gulped much
needed oxygen into her lungs. 'This isn't funny.'

'No,' he agreed solemnly, his hands trailing through
her hair and sending a slow shiver down her body. 'It's
deadly serious.'

'It——' his nearness was disarming her common sense
'—it's crazy.'

He nodded, watching her face intently. 'Definitely
crazy.'

A sigh tripped from her lips at the pleasure of his
fingers against her neck.

'You're so soft,' he whispered. 'So deliciously soft.'

Gently his hands moved themselves around her throat,
as if to strangle her, but she was afraid only of his
gentleness and the sensations it was detonating within
her. She knew that any second the wanton desire bub-
bling through her body would boil over into unleashed
passion. With her feeling as she did about this man, how
could it not?

His hands were now working their way down the
curves of her body, from breasts to waist to hips, in a
totally erotic fashion. She trembled.

'This isn't a good idea, Flanagan,' she muttered, opening her eyes and fighting against her body's desire to arch into his. 'We have to work together.'

'We work perfectly together.' He smiled lazily, nudging his hips against hers. 'Our bodies fit each other's like gloves.'

The arousal burning though her made her sigh a mixture of resignation and frustration. Her head drooped forward as his finger brushed across one aroused nipple then the other, and he was close enough to absorb her shuddered reaction to his touch.

'You want me, Jacqui,' he stated, his voice confident though raspy as he lifted her chin until her mouth was easily accessible to his. 'Every bit as much as I want you. *Here. Now.* All you have to do is tell me how fast or how slow you want to go...'

His words faded as his head inched nearer, then his tongue darted out to trail across her bottom lip in a slow, languid rhythm that went on and on long after Jacqui had opened her mouth to invite his entry.

'You set the pace, babe,' he whispered raggedly and, almost demented with the need to taste him, she instantly clamped her hands on either side of his head and assertively took possession of his mouth. His response was an earthy, satisfied groan as his arms locked around her waist and lifted her clear off the floor.

The feel and flavour of him after so long made her blood hum and heart dance, and breathing took a back seat to the aggressive ardour of their passion. When finally they drew apart their panting breaths came in unison, and their eyes were locked.

'I think choice just flew out the window,' he rasped, lowering her back to the floor in such a way that neither could ignore his aroused state. 'From my perspective it's got to be *hard* and *fast*. How about you?' His hand crept beneath her skirt and into the leg of her lacy panties.

Her slick wetness couldn't be denied. 'No arguments from me, Flanagan,' she whispered, her head lolling back in reflex response to the erotic titillation of his thumb.

'Ah, Jacqui,' he muttered against her neck, 'you're so damned exciting!'

In the next few moments Patric's mouth and hands managed to reduce her to sensual mindlessness as he disposed of her blouse and bra. Never had she wanted anything as urgently as she wanted this man, and the flames of her need burned so fiercely that she half expected to hear the shower-screen crack when her bare heated skin pressed against the hard coldness of the glass.

He released the waistband of her skirt with equal speed, and before the soft fabric had a chance to pool around her ankles her fingers were working feverishly to free him from his jeans.

She was almost crying with frustration—trust Flanagan to wear button-fly jeans rather than the zippered variety!—but he quickly came to her assistance, and such inane thoughts vanished as her fingers made contact with the pulsating length of him.

The tremor that quaked through Patric as her hand closed around him all but brought him to his knees. 'Oh, babe,' he gasped. 'You're playing with fire.'

'I know...' she said, lifting desire-dilated eyes to his. 'I want to burn with you, Patric.'

Her sex-roughened voice jerked at every muscle in his body, and as his arousal nudged against the smooth flatness of her belly he almost forgot the foil-covered condom he'd taken from his jeans. He took a ragged breath and showed it to her.

'I'm prepared this time,' he said. 'But if you're worried about last time, don't be. You're the only woman I've ever made love to without wearing protection.'

A shy blush tinted her cheeks, which, considering their situation, might have made him smile if he'd not ached so desperately for her. Slowly she reached to take the packet from him, but he shook his head.

'No way! If you put this on I'll probably explode in your hand.'

She grinned, obviously delighted to know the extent of her power over him. 'I wasn't going to put it on. I've only ever made love without one with *you*. But if *you're* concerned about practising safe sex——'

He groaned, and in one action lifted her against him until the gateway of her femininity was brushing his maleness. 'Honey, I don't think even protected sex between us could be called *safe*. Where we're concerned we're always on dangerous ground.'

Jacqui clutched at his shoulders as he drove into her, her satisfied purr harmonising with his more guttural groan of pleasure. Instinctively her legs went around his hips and her arms around his neck. The smile he gave her was arrogant and supremely sexy, but his words made it inoffensive.

'Lady, make sure *your* heart keeps beating, 'cause being inside you feels so good mine's stopped.'

In that instant Jacqui was certain that hers had too, but as she angled her head to meet his kiss the rhythm of his tongue, keeping perfect time with his thrusts, kick-started it again. Swamped by emotions and sensations, her body too picked up the tempo, and her last clear thought was that though typhoid could be cured she was beginning to think that what she felt for Patric Flanagan was terminal.

Legs bent, Patric leaned against the back of the spa-bath, providing an armchair-like support for Jacqui, positioned between his thighs. It didn't matter that her back was to him, for the mirror at the end of the tub reflected her face and other interesting parts of her anatomy with crystal-clearness.

'You're not going to sleep on me, are you?' he asked, stroking her cheek.

'No,' she said dreamily, then raised her lashes, letting her alert blue eyes meet his in the mirror. 'The last time I went to sleep after making love with you I woke up to find you gone.'

There was just enough accusation in her tone to prick his conscience. 'I thought the butterfly adorning your delicious rump meant that you were private property.'

He leaned forward to rest his chin on her shoulder, bringing their faces side by side, but his gaze was fixed on her mirror image. 'I don't like sharing,' he said firmly.

She smiled. 'Me neither.'

'Why did you tell me that Phil was your lover?'

She shook her head. 'I didn't. You *assumed* he was.'

'But you didn't correct that assumption. Why not?'

'It just seemed like a good idea not to. It made me feel...' she paused thoughtfully, slowly tracing her fingers from his ankles to his knees '...*safer*, I guess. Around you the air always seemed to be clogged with sexual tension.' She grinned. 'I felt like I was constantly skirting that "dangerous ground" you mentioned.'

'I think we'll have to re-signpost the area,' he muttered, trailing kisses across the width of her shoulders and finding the taste of her sweet beyond description.

'How does "heaven" sound as an alternative?' she suggested. Her hands were now caressing the insides of his thighs.

'Close to accurate.'

Her seductive smile, combined with her sleek, wet nakedness pressing against him, instantly stirred his lower body to life. She nestled still closer, her reflection revealing an impish grin. 'Ready for seconds, are we, Flanagan?'

He cupped the underside of her exposed breasts and gently teased the edges of her areolae until her nipples tightened to pebble hardness. A sultry purr of approval rolled from her lips.

'Yes, *Raynor*,' he said smugly into the mirror. 'I believe *we* are.'

'Raynomovski,' she corrected, splashing a wave of water on to the floor as she rolled over and hooked one arm around his neck.

'*Patric*,' he retorted, easing her body up until she straddled his lap.

'I've never called you Patric—*Flanagan*,' she said, massaging his chest with her free hand.

'Yes, you have.'

She frowned for a moment, then said, 'Oh, right, but that was in the first few minutes that I met you—when I was being the very socially acceptable Ms Jaclyn Raynor, Risqué Girl.'

'No. Since then.'

'Really? Well, I doubt if it'll ever happen again,' she told him, drawing ever decreasing circles around his nipples.

'Won't it?' he said.

'Nope. You see, you bring out my rough, inner-city roots. Besides,' she whispered against his mouth, 'Flanagan suits you better.'

Their kiss was the stuff of fireworks, but its flaming brilliance was quickly doused when they sank beneath the water. They came up, half spluttering, half giggling, and it was Flanagan who recovered first.

'Listen, honey, I might want to drown myself *in* you, but I sure as hell can't get off on the idea of drowning *with* you! What say we make use of that comfortable-looking queen-size in the other room?'

'I say——' Jacqui leapt from the tub '—last one in is on the bottom!'

She was draped across the bedspread with her long blonde plait wrapped seductively around her neck and over one breast when he reached the entrance of the room.

'What kept you, Flanagan?' she taunted.

'Your terms.'

His voice was husky with promise, making Jacqui's body throb as if he'd touched her. Then, in what seemed like one smooth movement, he was on the mattress, lifting her over him and carefully licking the droplets of water from her skin.

She arched back as his tongue laved first one breast and then the other, whimpering with desire as his oral adoration progressed to a suckling tug, a cross between torture and bliss, which brought searing heat to her loins—a heat that steamed her blood and fogged her brain.

She fought to position herself on to him, but he held her firmly short of her much needed goal, creating an ever tightening knot in the core of her. His ministrations went on and on, tightening and tightening the strands of desire within her, until she was squirming in frustration against his hand and his knowingly teasing thumb, effectively torturing herself.

'Now,' she pleaded. 'I want you now!' He pulled her forward and plunged his tongue between her teeth in an imitation of what she wanted. All the time his hands were promising heaven but leaving her in front of its gates.

'Please,' she muttered, knowing that she wanted him inside her when she convulsed with love for him. 'I...ah! I...want you with me, Patric.'

'Say it again.'

She heard his rasped command from a million miles away as he propelled her closer and closer to nirvana. She shook her head. 'No!' she shouted. 'No, Patric, I want you with me!'

His entry was quick and gratifying.

'I'm with you, babe! Ah, honey...' he said, showering kisses over her face. 'I'm...with you...all the way!'

In her heart Jacqui acknowledged that she would never have enough of this man; at the same time her mind acknowledged that she mightn't have him for long. So, taking advantage of her superior position, and spurred on by her love for him, she rode her emotions as frantically as if this was the last chance she'd have to love him. She toppled over the edge of sensuality only seconds after she felt his warm release.

She'd been right to label what she felt for Flanagan as terminal, for now she knew with heart-quivering certainty that she would die loving this man.

CHAPTER THIRTEEN

THE motion of Patric's hand up and down her sweat-slicked spine alerted Jacqui to the fact that he was awake. Resting her head on his chest, she walked two fingers along his upper arm.

'If that's how you react when I call you by your Christian name, I'm definitely going to stick to Flanagan in public.'

She felt his silent chuckle.

'I'm comfortable with that,' he murmured, tracing the spot on her hip that bore the tattoo.

'That's the proof of my misspent youth. I got it as a dare and have hated it ever since,' she said.

'Don't. I think it's as sexy as hell—like the woman who has it.'

'Well, you've *nearly* convinced me it's not a turn-off for you. But I might need more proof later,' she teased.

He groaned and propped himself on one elbow to look at her. 'How much later? We males hit our sexual peak at eighteen, you know.'

She rolled off him, grinning. 'Then you must be a real *late* developer, Flanagan!'

'I think the incentive has a lot to do with it. You're one helluva lady.'

'One helluva *hungry* lady! Want to give room service a try?'

'I think we should talk first.'

The sudden seriousness of his voice clued Jacqui in to what was coming, and she immediately fought to rally her emotions.

'Is this where you remind me about your aversion to models and tell me how I mustn't get any ideas about this being a lasting relationship?'

'Something like that.' He sighed. 'Jacqui, if you'd been anything but a model we'd have been lovers long before this——'

'Said he arrogantly,' she cut in, smiling not only to take the sting from her words but to convince herself that she wasn't afraid of what was coming next.

'What I mean is that I was attracted to you from the moment I saw you, but your being a model made me automatically dismiss that there could be anything more than a business relationship between us.'

'That and the belief that I'd been sleeping with your father.'

'Yeah, well, that kind of goes hand in hand with how I felt about models in general.'

'I thought it was something to do with your mother?'

'That too. But she wasn't the only woman who screwed up my life.'

Suddenly it seemed imperative to stall off whatever it was he was going to say. She didn't want to hear about the other women in his life. OK, maybe a sick part of her did—but not *now*! Not when her body still carried the imprints of his lovemaking and the dampness of his sweat.

'Flanagan,' she said, trying for lightness, 'are you *sure* we can't order something to eat *now*? This sounds like it's going to be a long story, with an awful lot of sub-plots.'

'It is,' he said, giving his attention to the solitary braid of her hair for several moments before lifting his gaze back to her face. 'But I want you to know where I'm coming from.' He gave his head a sudden shake. 'It's important that you do.'

Jacqui could no more have refused to listen than she could refuse to love him. She nodded to show that she was listening, but it was several minutes before Flanagan started to speak.

'My mother was born dirt-poor but incredibly beautiful, and those two factors obsessively drove her life for as long as I can remember. She grew up being told that her looks would be her ticket out of poverty, and she made fame her destination.'

'I've seen some of the albums Wade had of her. Her trip was certainly a success.'

Flanagan didn't smile at her pun as she'd intended; instead, an almost remote sadness invaded his profile.

'Except she never knew when to get off the train. Or considered how her actions might affect the people close to her.'

'Like you and Wade?' she ventured softly. When he said nothing she added, 'He never said so, but I got the impression that Wade loved her very much.'

Beside her, Flanagan made a disparaging sound. 'He loved her and he hated her,' he said. 'I'm still not sure which was the more dominant emotion, but then, I spent more time in boarding-school than I ever did with either of them.'

'What about vacations? You must have at least come home then.'

'Sure. But that didn't mean *they* were home.' He seemed hypnotised by the motion of his thumb over her knuckles as he spoke. 'One or the other was usually away on some shoot, and on the rare occasion when the three of us were together I felt like I was in the middle of World War III.'

He stopped playing with her hand and lifted his eyes to her face, as if for an instant he hadn't been sure why he was telling her this and didn't want to continue. Seeing the hurt, haunted look tensing his face, Jacqui had intended to tell him not to say any more, but she surprised herself by saying, 'Go on.'

'My parents married after what I gather was a short, torrid affair in Europe, during which my father launched Madelene's career and consolidated his already rapid rise in the photographic world.

'For a few years they were both happy with their fast-paced lives, but Dad was from a conservative, wealthy Irish background and had a strong desire—not to mention a lot of pressure put on him—to have a family.

Madelene flatly refused. Kids weren't on her agenda under any circumstances; fame was her passion, money her idol and pregnancy her worst nightmare.'

'So you're adopted?'

He seemed momentarily startled that she should have drawn that conclusion, before an ironic smile formed on his mouth. 'No, I'm a classic example of how unreliable birth-control can be.'

'Oh. I'm sorry.'

'Why?' His expression was pure puzzlement.

'Well, I guess it must be kind of hard to grow up knowing you were an...an accident.'

'At least I'm here,' he said dully. 'Madelene told me more than once that if she hadn't been Catholic she'd have had me aborted——'

'Oh, my God!' Jacqui's gasp held genuine shock. 'How could a mother say that to a child?'

'Madelene was nothing if not brutally honest,' he said bitterly. 'She saw child-bearing as a threat to her career—something to avoid at all costs. She arranged to have a tubal ligation immediately after my birth without even consulting my father.

'Years later, when they were having a fight because he wanted her to quit modelling and consider having another child, she threw it up at him. That's when Wade started having affairs, and from then on the marriage—like Madelene's career—was pretty much all over bar the shouting.'

His mouth twisted into an ironic sneer. 'Actually the shouting outlasted everything—even the divorce.'

'Was that when she went back to Canada?' He nodded. 'But why did...?' She paused, trying to think of a tactful way of asking what puzzled her. She needn't have bothered; he read her mind.

'Why did I go with her?'

'Yeah. I mean, given the way she treated you——'

'In her own way Madelene loved me. Oh, she mightn't have loved me from birth, with that instinctive maternal love all women are supposed to have, but she grew to love me. And she was usually fine with me if Wade wasn't around.'

'Wade deliberately came between you?'

'It wasn't deliberate. And it wasn't only Wade. You see, if there was an adult male present—*any* adult male— it was *his* attention, *his* approval and *his* affection that Madelene needed. It wasn't intentional, it was just Madelene. She needed reassurance that her face and body were every bit as fabulous as they'd always been.

'When they weren't, and her work started drying up, she took to drinking—*heavily*. Champagne was her preferred beverage, from sun-up to sundown. The only time she even tried to stay sober was when I was around, carefully saying all the things she wanted to hear and making her laugh.'

'How old were you?'

'Fifteen,' he said flatly. 'But I felt fifty. Still, for all her faults Madelene was still my mother, and, as my being around seemed to have a positive effect on her, when she asked me to move to Canada with her I said yes.'

'How did Wade react to that?'

'He thought it was the best thing to do. He still cared about Madelene; maybe he even still loved her—I don't know—but he'd given up trying to deal with her years before.' He paused and ran a weary hand over his face, and her heart felt his pain.

'Not a happy story, huh?' His question was a carelessly intoned rhetorical one, but when he turned his face into her hand and kissed her palm the urge to comfort him was so overwhelming that Jacqui nearly wept.

'Strange, isn't it?' she said, caressing his slightly scratchy jaw. 'I grew up thinking that kids with backgrounds like yours must be so lucky—that poverty was the only thing that could hurt anyone.'

His chuckle chilled her to the bone.

'Honey, you were right! Take it from me, *poverty* not money is the root of all evil.' At her stunned look he patted her hand. 'Relax, I'm being deliberately cynical—

but you have to hear the second half of the story to understand why. And, believe me, it's no better than the first.'

Trepidation began sliding along her nerve-endings. 'I'm not sure I want to hear it,' she said honestly.

'It'll help explain why I've been fighting my feelings for you for so long.' He searched her face with frank brown eyes. 'And why I still am to some extent.'

Something in his gaze turned her heart into an ice-cube, chilling her to her toes. 'If this is a brush-off, Flanagan, I'd rather have it straight.'

'It's not a brush-off,' he said solemnly. 'In fact, if I didn't think this relationship was going to run for longer than a few sessions of hot, torrid sex, I wouldn't be telling you this.'

Her temperature soared back towards boiling-point, but she dipped her head, sensing that it wasn't wise to let him see the depth of her feelings for him.

He guided her chin up. 'I *need* to tell you.'

That simple statement dangled untouched in the surrounding silence for what seemed an eternity. Jacqui searched his face in the hope that his need was based in love for her, not selfishness. She found no answer either way.

She sighed, resigning herself to the knowledge that she'd never be able to deny this man anything he believed that he needed.

'OK, Flanagan,' she said, injecting lightness into her voice. 'Give me Part Two—but, be advised, if you have any aspirations of having your life story turned into a movie, forget them! I suspect a six-part mini-series wouldn't do it justice!'

His smile was gentle. 'Both ideas would bomb—simply because there isn't an actress around who's beautiful enough to play you.'

Jacqui was fleetingly hopeful that the look he sent her meant that his passion might spare her having to listen to what she suspected was going to be painful. Certainly painful for her. But his kiss, though tender, was quickly over, and he rolled away from her to stare at the ceiling.

'I met Angelica when I was studying photography at college. A pal introduced us, saying that she was looking for a part-time modelling job to earn enough money to undertake a photography course.

'Angel—as she liked to be called—was uniquely and breathtakingly beautiful, and any fool could have seen that she was more suited to the other side of a lens, so I asked if she'd considered it. She said no, because she couldn't afford to have a portfolio done, so I said I'd do one free of charge. That's when her eyes lit up like neon signs and I fell instantly in love!'

The jealousy Jacqui felt towards the unknown woman tasted like acid in her mouth, and she had to force herself to listen as Flanagan continued.

'We started dating, but I had no idea how different our backgrounds were until a couple of weeks later, when I was invited to have dinner with her family. Once I'd seen the appalling surroundings she lived in I asked her to move in with me. At first she was reluctant, saying she wouldn't feel right living in sin, no matter how much she loved me. So I proposed.'

'And suddenly her morals flew out the window?' Jacqui's question was rhetorical—she already knew the answer—but she was given confirmation of it.

'Man, I was so dumb!' The obvious self-contempt in Flanagan's voice provided her with a small measure of satisfaction. 'Besotted idiot that I was, I practically threw my money at her—not to mention at the rest of her family.'

'But surely you couldn't have been earning that much?'

He looked at her as if she were stupid, then blinked and said, 'Oh, I guess I forgot to explain about my grandparents.'

She nodded.

'When my parents divorced, my Irish grandparents disinherited Wade, and since his twin brother had died single a few years earlier I inherited their scientific publishing empire when they died.'

Wade had never told Jacqui about his background, so this was something of a surprise. 'So you're saying you were putrid rich back then?'

'I still am,' he told her shortly.

'I...I had no idea.'

'No? Well, I'm a lot smarter now than I was when I met Angel. I don't advertise my wealth and I don't delude myself that money buys happiness or any other intangible human emotion.

'Unfortunately I wasn't so wise at twenty, and, when Angel protested about how guilty she'd feel living in luxury while her parents were unemployed and barely able to pay the rent, I thought, What the heck? I was in love, and it wasn't as if I couldn't afford to make her happy!

'So I did what any lovesick idiot would do—bought a new home for her parents in an upmarket area and set her father up in a trucking business. No strings attached!'

Jacqui was speechless, but she knew that her feelings showed in her face.

'You can't think me any more of a fool than I do myself,' he told her. 'Suckers didn't come any bigger than me back then!

'Anyway, I put a portfolio of her together and she sent it to every high-profile agency in New York and the offers flooded in. Angel accepted the highest-paying one, although my gut feeling was to go with one offering slightly less but with a more solid reputation. But Angel was big on making her own decisions, and she disregarded my advice and opinions on her career as glibly as she disregarded them on everything else.'

'But you gave her her start,' Jacqui protested. 'And your background automatically gave you more insight into the industry than she'd have had. Heavens, both your parents were icons in the business!'

'Which was exactly why—as I found out much later— Angel had engineered our meeting in the first place.' He swore. 'I was played for a fool, and I not only smiled while it happened, but *paid* for it into the bargain!'

She wanted to say that it had been Angelica not he who'd been the fool. How could a woman who'd already had Flanagan's love have needed more? Wanted any more?

'I'll never make the same mistake again. I wouldn't be that stupid twice.'

The sadness in his face tore at her, and desperately she grabbed at words that would reassure him that *she* didn't think he was stupid. She wanted to tell him that she thought he was the smartest, most wonderful man she'd ever known, and that she loved him beyond belief. But she couldn't. Because at this moment she knew that he wouldn't let himself believe in such a love. In fact she feared that he never would.

Trying to rise above her own despair, she searched for a way to reduce his, to bring the devilish, light-hearted Flanagan grin back to his face. She swallowed once and forced a smile.

'So look on the bright side, Flanagan,' she said glibly. 'They reckon you can't put a price on experience, but with a good accountant you could probably come pretty close to it!'

His reaction told her that he hadn't taken her words in the spirit she'd intended. He jumped off the bed, uttering a string of expletives.

'I'm sorry... I...' Her voice died under the weight of his quick, stabbing glare, before he turned, fists clenched, to face the wall.

The anger and tension bracing his muscles were highlighted by his nudity. Oh, God, Jacqui thought, what had this woman done to him?

She wanted to go to him and got off the bed, but was too afraid of doing more damage than her wise-cracking mouth already had, and instead stood silently beside him. The atmosphere of the room became utterly still and chilled by the invisible wall which Patric had stepped behind—a wall of silence and remoteness so impregnable that Jacqui knew any breach in it would have to come from Patric.

When he did finally speak it startled her, but there was no trace of rage in his voice now, and she let out the breath she'd been unaware of holding.

'Three days before we were due to marry I walked in and overheard Angel telling her mother that she'd cancelled an appointment she'd made at a well-known termination clinic.'

Jacqui's blood ran cold. 'She... she was pregnant?'

He sneered, shaking his head. 'She'd *thought* she was. It turned out to be what *she* called "a false alarm". She'd only been four days late with her period, but the thought of pregnancy jeopardising her precious career had had her lining up abortionists before she'd even bothered to have her condition confirmed!'

He swore violently and punched the wall. 'The bitch hadn't even been going to tell me! We were to have married in a few days, yet she'd have aborted our child because it would have interrupted her career!' He ran both hands through his hair. 'Like I said, Madelene wasn't real maternal, but at least she gave me the chance to breathe.'

Tears blurred Jacqui's vision and she bit down hard on her hand to stop the sob in her throat from escaping. No wonder he hated models! The two most important women in his life had put their careers before him. Between them they'd made him feel as if his life and the possible life of his future child were worth less than a *job*—a job which at best might span twelve years.

'It really makes my gut churn to know my judgement is so lousy, that I could have imagined myself in love with such a manipulative little tramp in the first place,' he continued. 'To her I was a meal ticket and a rung on the ladder of success. Since then I've been wary of career women in general and models in particular.'

His self-recrimination clawed at Jacqui's heart and she threw her arms around him. 'Oh, Flanagan...' Her intention had been to console him, but it was he who became the comforter as tides of silent tears ran down her face and on to his chest.

As Patric held the warm, quietly sobbing woman in his arms he realised that her distress was even more unbearable to him than his memories. Ah, hell! Why hadn't he remembered that Phil had told him Jacqui had been present at her nephew's birth? His timing was lousy! No wonder she was so damned upset.

Cursing his selfish insensitivity, he lifted her into his arms and carried her back to the bed. Burying his face in the silkiness of her hair, he held her tightly until her sobs abated and her body was again relaxed and pliant against him.

'Feeling better?' he asked, when a tear-streaked face tried to smile at him.

The waves of relief that washed over him at her nod were accompanied by a silent prayer of thanks. Yet he was uncomfortably aware of the remnants of high-density emotion lingering in the room. Anxious to escape its cloying effects, he dropped a kiss on Jacqui's nose and suggested the first thing that came into his head.

'Let's hit the beach for a few hours,' he said.

'Wait,' she said urgently as he moved away from her.

The confusion and indecision troubling her face made him uneasy. 'What is it?'

'Flanagan, you said that you can't trust birth-control to be one hundred per cent reliable. You also implied that your judgement wasn't to be trusted.' She looked at him for confirmation.

'Yeah. So?' Damn her! He didn't want to discuss this any more! Couldn't she just let it go? Hell, he'd already told her more than he'd ever told anyone else.

'So, no one's judgement is one hundred per cent trustworthy,' she said earnestly. 'But has it never occurred to you that yours is worth more than it ever was now that you've learned there's no such thing as a wingless angel?'

CHAPTER FOURTEEN

TWENTY-FIVE minutes later Jacqui was almost surprised to discover that there was nothing to distinguish them from the scores of other couples and families frolicking under the mid-afternoon sun on Port Macquarie's most popular beach. And she revelled in the ordinariness of being with Flanagan for a reason other than one which pertained to their business arrangement.

Sitting cross-legged on their towels, they sipped cola and ate sauce-drenched Pluto pups—batter-covered frankfurters on sticks—which Flanagan claimed he hadn't had for 'a hundred years'.

Then, while waiting a sensible period before finishing their food and swimming, they joked and talked about inane topics such as their star signs and what football teams they followed. Politically they were poles apart, but, considering how Flanagan seemed not even to notice the appreciative glances being directed at him by practically every female between the ages of five and ninety-five, Jacqui was prepared to forgive him anything!

However, on a public beach the silent message he sent her with his eyes as they roamed possessively over her body, and the way he kept finding reasons to touch her, became a form of torture. In lieu of a cold shower she finally jumped to her feet and sprinted towards the water's edge, knowing that he was in pursuit.

Physically exhausted after their madcap antics in the surf, she lay face down on her towel, revelling in the feel of masculine hands animating her skin with sunscreen. But, though the firm, slow movement of Flanagan's fingers across the muscles of her shoulders and back felt nearly as therapeutic as it did seductive, it did little to ease her mental tension.

For, while it had been easy for a time to lose herself in the energy of the light-hearted, teasingly boyish Flanagan, who'd made her laugh until she'd almost drowned, then had insisted on giving her his version of the kiss of life in water so deep that she'd had to wrap herself around him to stay afloat, a part of her mind was still dwelling on the anguish she'd heard in his voice back in the hotel room.

'Relax,' she was told as male fingers kneaded the curves between her shoulders and neck. 'Don't waste your beautiful vitality dwelling on my past problems.'

Startled at how easily he'd read her mind, Jacqui tried to turn, but gentle pressure from him discouraged it.

'I . . . I'm not,' she lied.

'Good! 'Cause, believe me, my scars have healed . . .'

That's what you think, Patric Flanagan, she responded mentally.

'I didn't tell you about Angelica to upset you or milk you for sympathy——'

'I know that!' Again she tried to roll over, but he prevented her.

'Shh,' he commanded. 'Let me talk.'

Sighing mutinously, she propped her chin back on her forearms and Flanagan resumed both his massage and his speech.

'Hon', even though you've made me realise all models aren't like my mother and Angelica, I'd be lying if I said I still didn't have misgivings about our relationship.'

Beneath his fingers, she willed herself not to react physically to his words.

'However,' he went on, 'I'd like for us to continue being lovers as well as business partners. I'm not sure it'll work, but I'd like to try. But *only*,' he said quickly and with emphasis, 'if you're prepared to accept that it's a one-day-at-a-time deal, without promises or expectations.' His hands stilled. 'Are you?'

Her pride shouted *no*! Her heart yelled *yes*! And though her mind recognised the internal war her body, glorying under Flanagan's touch, declared it no contest.

Oh, sure, he was only offering a short-term affair while she craved long-term commitment, but it was better than anything she'd hoped to hear from him, and a billion times more than anything she'd ever want to hear from another man. Put simply, she loved Flanagan so much that she'd have him any way she could.

He interrupted her thoughts to add, 'Of course, regardless of your decision—or of how things turn out—our business contract will still stand. But that's the only promise I'm willing to give you.'

Honestly, he was so thick at times that she could have thumped him! Did he really think that she was worried about how this would affect their business arrangement? She wanted to tell him that all the money in the world couldn't have made her love him any more than she already did, but to have done so would have had him retreating at the speed of light, so she didn't.

'I haven't asked for promises,' she whispered, sifting a handful of sand between trembling fingers.

'I know. But I have to be sure that you understand this isn't going to last forever.'

'I understand. It'll last until you end it.'

She was turned gently on to her back. 'Or you,' he said.

He'd missed the subtle phrasing of her words. She wasn't sure if she was glad or sorry.

'Whatever,' she muttered.

The flavour of dried salt-water on his lips and the intensity of his kiss were like a drug, the side effects of which on Jacqui were a rapidly quickening pulse and a slow, melting sensation in her loins. She wrapped her arms around his neck, marvelling at the suppressed power of his muscled shoulders and the sensuality of his oil-slicked hands skimming down her thighs. With her body's need for him escalating by the second, the groan she gave at the sudden departure of his lips from hers was a combination of arousal and complaint.

'Honey,' he whispered huskily into her ear, 'there are two things I like about you over every other model I've ever known.'

His tongue laved her ear and she sighed, twisting her head to grant him more access to her neck. 'What are they?'

'Firstly,' he said, dampening her lobe in the most provocative way, 'you're dynamite in the sack.' He groaned and quickly rolled away when her mouth tried to copy the action of his. 'Not to mention on a public beach!'

She grinned. 'And secondly?'

'You're established in your career and financially independent. These days I like to know my woman is debt-free. So,' he smirked, 'want to go back to our room and discuss the first of your good points in detail?'

Jacqui nodded vigorously. She sure didn't want to discuss the second any time soon!

It was two weeks later when Jacqui aimed her camera at Flanagan, who was carefully inspecting the bent front wheel-guard on his trail-bike.

When he'd complained because she wouldn't allow him to take candid photos of her—especially as he had no intention of including them in his book—it had occurred to Jacqui that while the finished book would always be a reminder of her time with Flanagan, it wouldn't include photographs of him. More than anything she wanted tangible evidence—even if it was only two-dimensional—of the man who'd brought her heart and body to fulfilment.

So, hiding behind a façade of feminism, she'd argued that unless he could accept that what was good for the goose was good for the gander he could forget taking anything but professional photographs of her! Reluctantly he'd agreed to a trade-off, and so far Jacqui had gone through nearly four rolls of film.

Finally satisfied with her focus, she fired off three quick shots of him crouched beside the wheel of the bike.

'Jacqui,' he said, with mock exasperation, rising to his full height. 'It'd be more help if your aspirations lay in the panel-beating field rather than photography. I can do that myself.'

She wrinkled her nose at him, then put the camera back in the car.

'You know,' he said, his muscles bunching as he lifted the bike on to the rack at the back of the Land Rover and secured it. 'If anyone had told me that the sophisticated Risque Girl was a bike nut I'd have laughed at them.'

This was the third time that they'd been off-road riding together, but the memory of how stunned Flanagan had looked when on the first occasion Jacqui had jumped on the bike and executed a wheel-stand and several other, more fancy tricks was something she'd never forget, even if she didn't have it on film.

'Let's face it, Flanagan, publicising that the woman was who supposed to epitomise femininity to the nth degree had grown up hanging out with a group of bikers wouldn't have been a shrewd marketing move.'

'Oh, I don't know,' he said. 'I think you look incredibly sexy wearing dirt-caked jeans and bikers boots astride a trail-bike.'

'You don't look so bad yourself, Flanagan,' she retorted, not even attempting to avoid the male arms which reached around her waist and held her tight. 'Although I can't wait to see you on that Harley you're having shipped from Canada. A customised Hog definitely suits your macho image a lot better.' She smiled. 'And, don't forget, you promised me a ride.'

'Oh, I won't!' he vowed, lifting a hand to the flesh exposed by the opening of her blouse. 'I find the idea of you straddling something masculine and powerful more than appeals to me.' His finger snaked lower, dipping into her cleavage, and that, plus the scorching look in his eyes, had white heat coiling through her abdomen.

'Too bad the Harley isn't here, huh?'

Instantly his hand moved to the back of her neck and brought her mouth level with his. 'Who said I was talking about the Hog, honey?' he said against her lips.

Enclosed in the strong male arms holding her hard against his body, Jacqui felt like the most desired woman in the world, yet at the same time like a cherished, protected child. She wondered how a man could possibly make a woman experience two such sexual extremes at the same time, then gave up.

It was useless to try and analyse the power of Flanagan's wizardry; all she could do was accept it— accept that just as no man had previously evoked the sensations and emotions Flanagan did none ever would again. But it stunned her that, in the wake of the number of times they'd made love, a kiss alone should affect her so profoundly.

He drew back slightly and she saw his handsomeness through a blur of desire as he cupped her face, then she closed her eyes, wanting only to concentrate on the seductive gentleness of his thumbs grazing her lips... her cheekbones... her eyebrows...

He exhaled a ragged breath. 'I have a suggestion to make,' he said suggestively.

Recalling the lovemaking which had followed their picnic lunch earlier that day, and the blanket lying only metres from them, Jacqui sighed. 'Hmm?'

'Let's pack up the rest of the stuff and head back to the hotel.'

She tried to conceal her disappointment, but with her brain cloudy from his kisses and caresses her execution wasn't good.

'Don't look like that,' he urged, the hands on her face now still.

'Sorry,' she muttered, then forced a smile. 'I guess it has been a long day.'

He pressed more firmly against her cheeks. 'It hasn't been a *long* day. For me it's been a *wonderful* day. Ah, honey.' He sighed and hugged her close. 'I want you so much I ache! But it's getting late.'

'So?' she said, petulant despite the pleasure she felt at his words.

'So——' he winked down at her '—I want you slow and gentle, and I don't want darkness hiding your body from me when I love you.'

Her aroused moan was caught in his mouth, but this time his kiss was exquisitely tender, stirring her love rather than her passion. When he lifted his mouth from hers Jacqui knew that the instant smile she gave him was genuine—she felt it burst from her heart.

That night she awoke from the satiated slumber she'd drifted into after Flanagan had delivered on his promise of slow, gentle loving. From the feel of the even male breath breezing against her shoulder she knew that her lover was sound asleep, and she stretched carefully to flick off the bedside lamp, plunging the room into darkness.

When they'd first discussed Flanagan's idea for his pictorial on Australian beauty spots, he'd told Jacqui that she could expect a total of three weeks of location work to fulfil her commitments to the project. But if Flanagan had been worried that the schedule he'd arranged for their stay on the New South Wales north coast had already run a week over time he'd hidden it well. Not that the shoots they'd done had been troublesome and consumed more time than necessary—quite the contrary.

The acceptance and ongoing exploration of the physical attraction they shared had made Jacqui utterly uninhibited about posing nude, and if progress had been slower than planned it was only because she and Patric had become too easily lured into doing spontaneous things, such as sharing candlelit dinners, spending days at the beach or, like today, trail-bike riding and, of course, making fantastically beautiful love.

And, on Jacqui's part, she was falling deeper and deeper in love with each rapidly passing day.

Now, viewing the room's darkness through wet lashes and tearful eyes, Jacqui wished again that the heady cocktail of love and hope which kept her drunk with happiness during the daylight hours could be equally potent at night. It was only at times like this, awake on her own in the darkness, that she felt the claws of guilt gouging at her.

She wasn't the debt-free success that Flanagan thought her. Far from it. She'd intended to tell him the truth a hundred times, but somehow there had always seemed too many reasons not to.

Originally she'd decided that what Flanagan didn't know couldn't hurt him—though all too quickly that had become a case of what Flanagan didn't know couldn't hurt *her*.

It had been when she'd discovered that clichés couldn't salve a guilty conscience that she'd started trying to justify her omission of the truth by telling herself that it wasn't really any of his business!

They were *lovers*, not a married couple with a joint bank account. And since Flanagan had been the one to request the no-commitment clause in their relationship she should hardly be expected to reveal her personal financial situation to him!

And now? Well, now it was far too late...

Feeling again the rush of dread she'd experienced when over dinner Flanagan had announced that he thought they should begin the trip back to Sydney the day after tomorrow, Jacqui swallowed down a sob. Though he'd said nothing about ending their affair, she was afraid that, once removed from the idyllic, ironically honeymoon-like state in which it had existed during the last few weeks, their relationship would crash and die.

A shiver skipped down her spine, and desperately she snuggled deeper into the warmth of Flanagan, whose arm even in sleep tightened possessively around her.

No! She simply wasn't prepared to jeopardise even one precious second of what little time she had left with this man. It was entirely likely that if she explained now he'd think she'd agreed to an affair as a means of convincing him to bail her out of debt! She couldn't take that chance. Not yet.

Besides, when she received the money due to her for this assignment she *would* be debt-free! Finally and completely. Then she would explain everything to Flanagan... She would even tell him that she loved him.

Tension and the uncertain light of dusk filled Jacqui's living-room two days later as Flanagan lowered her luggage to the floor.

'That's the last of it,' he announced unnecessarily, his eyes looking everywhere but at her.

'Th-thank you,' she stammered, feeling awkward beneath his thoughtful gaze, yet deserted when he turned it away.

'What are you doing tomorrow?' He appeared to be asking the photograph on her cork board, but she answered anyway.

'Nothing,' she said, smiling eagerly. 'What would you like to do?'

He turned back to her, a slight frown marring his forehead as if he *had* actually been speaking to the photographs.

'Huh? Nothing. What I mean is,' he said quickly, 'I'll be in the dark-room most of the day.'

'Oh, right. Of course,' she said, as evenly as her disappointment would allow.

'How about I bring the developed prints over tomorrow evening? We can discuss how they came out. I figure you're as eager as I am to see them.'

It wasn't the damn photographs she cared about seeing, it was *him*. And if he didn't realise that by now then she was going to leave him in no doubt about it tomorrow night! Smiling, she started to visualise the scene she would set... For starters she would dress as sexily as she knew how, and she'd have scented candles burning, soft music playing in the background, a romantic dinner...

'Jacqui?' he questioned, pulling her from her daze. 'Did you hear what I said?'

'What? Oh, yeah.' She smiled provocatively up at him. 'If you give me some idea of what time you'll be here I'll toss in a complimentary dinner.'

He sighed wearily. 'Babe, the way I am at the moment, schedules are the last thing I can think about keeping to. Better for you if you just expect me when you see me, and don't go putting yourself to any extra trouble for my benefit.' He took the kind of breath that made one expect a long monologue to follow, but instead he just grimaced. 'Sorry, hon'.'

His message was all too loud, clear and heart-breaking. Tears began to well in her eyes but she fought to quell them.

'No, that's fine! Really! I...I'll just...expect you when I see you,' she said glibly. 'And I won't be surprised if I don't. I know how busy you are——'

'Oh, I'll definitely be here.' His tone seemed vague and distracted. 'There's a lot we have to discuss, such as——'

'I'm going to have a cup of coffee!' Her interruption was swift and desperate. She didn't want to hear him say, Such as our relationship. 'You're welcome to stay,' she continued. Then as his head started to shake added, 'For coffee, I mean! Just for coffee!' She felt like an absolute fool. She'd suddenly become so conscious of not saying the wrong thing that she was making things worse.

'Thanks, but no. Like I said, I'm worn out after the trip, and in more need of a decent night's sleep than caffeine.'

His implication that she was the cause of his sleep deprivation was anything but subtle! Huh! *She* wasn't the one who'd instigated what had practically been an endurance marathon last night!

'I know how you feel,' she said agreeably. 'I can't re-member the last time *I* got a decent night's sleep.'

She ignored his frown and walked into the kitchen to fill the electric jug and switch it on.

She was determined not to say another word until he did, which might be never—he'd hardly been receptive to conversation, much less inclined to instigate it, at any stage of their drive home!

And he'd offered no explanation as to why ten minutes after they'd got in the Land Rover he'd announced that he was aborting his original plan of a leisurely three-day return via the New England tablelands and opting for a straight stint along the Pacific Highway. Jacqui, coward that she was, and fearing his answer, hadn't asked.

Feeling his eyes on her, but steadfastly refusing to meet his gaze, she set about placing everything that she needed for coffee on the bench. Her taut nerves stretched tighter and tighter, until she became terminally clumsy and was chinking mugs and juggling the sugar bowl like a drunken octopus.

When the teaspoon slid from her fingers it clanged into the stainless-steel sink with a pitch high enough to break the sound barrier, but it wasn't until she opened the refrigerator and realised that there was no fresh milk that her frustration became too much. She swore violently.

'What's up?' he asked.

'There's no milk!' she shouted, as if it was somehow his fault.

'Want me to run down and borrow some from your sister?'

'No! I'm more than capable of doing it myself. Besides, I thought you were going home?'

'I am. I just wanted to make sure you were OK by yourself.'

'Why wouldn't I be, for God's sake?'

'No reason.' He straightened. 'Well, I'd better get going. I'll give you a call tomorrow, OK?'

She nodded, hating how bored he sounded. Even the kiss he gave her lacked his usual attention and enthusiasm.

'Night, babe,' he whispered. 'I'll see you tomorrow.'

Jacqui watched him go until he had vanished beyond the hedge of the tennis court, then slid the glass door shut and closed the curtains. Silent, scalding tears slipped down her face.

What she'd most feared was becoming a reality. It was coming to an end. A loud cry ripped from her throat as a more terrifying thought gripped her... Perhaps Flanagan thought it was already over...

CHAPTER FIFTEEN

As JACQUI had expected, the photographs turned out to be brilliant. What she hadn't expected, after the way they'd parted company the previous evening, was the manner in which Flanagan had swept her into his arms the moment she'd opened the door; or the wonderful, erotic love they'd made until the early hours of the morning.

Yet, after more than twenty-four hours of tearfully preparing herself for his announcement that their no-promises affair had reached its end, her elation at discovering that she was a certifiable pessimist thrilled her!

Now, with soft morning sun filtering into her room, she lovingly ran her hands over the sleeping body of the man who graced her bed. She wasn't sure how long the reprieve would last, but she wasn't going to torture herself by analysing his every word and action.

She gasped when her hand was entrapped at the same instant as a sleepily sexy male gaze locked with hers.

'I didn't intend to stay all night,' he said, dragging his free hand through the length of her unsecured hair. 'But I'm glad I did.'

She smiled and lowered herself on to his chest. 'Me too, Flanagan.'

Their kiss started out as languidly as the sun drifted through the bedroom window, but its heat rose far more rapidly, filling the air with muted moans and whispered endearments which made sense only to them. Eager hands and lips fed the fires of their need, until further attempts to forestall the natural culmination of their passion would have been as useless as trying to halt the dawn.

Except on the first occasion, their lovemaking had never been silent, but when Flanagan rose quickly from the bed, and with no thought of afterplay headed to the bathroom, Jacqui feared that this time she'd gone too far. Dammit! She wasn't sure whether she'd told him she loved him or not!

Cooking breakfast, she tried desperately to forget what she'd felt and recall exactly what she'd said...*aloud*, but to no avail. The only thing she *was* certain of was that Flanagan *hadn't* said he loved her!

He was brooding and distracted when he joined her in the kitchen, and she forced false gaiety into her voice. 'Hi, ready for breakfast?'

'There's something I want to discuss first,' he said grimly.

'Sounds ominous. How many guesses do I get?' She'd get through this on banter, she told herself.

'I've decided I'm not going to use the photographs of you in the book.'

'But...but you agreed they were good. Exactly what you wanted.'

'I changed my mind.'

'Oh? Well.' She smiled. 'I guess I can stand to shoot them again.

'You don't understand, Jacqui,' he said. 'I don't want you in the book. Your modelling assignment is finished. I'm freeing you of all obligations to me, and vice versa.'

Pain scorched her soul, and she had to grip on to the sink to avoid buckling to the ground. Oh, God, why hadn't she been able to keep her big, stupid mouth shut? If she'd kept her deepest feelings from him she might at least have had his friendship—if not his passion—until the end of the assignment. But he was so determined to end their involvement that even that wasn't a possibility.

The thought of absolute, cold-turkey withdrawal from Flanagan terrified her. She couldn't do it. *He* couldn't do it to her. She wouldn't let him!

'You can't do that Flanagan; we have a contract!'

'I'm going to tear it up.'

'The hell you are!' she raged. 'I'll...I'll sue you for every cent you have if you so much as try it!' She ignored his surprised expression, driven on by her churning emotions. 'Our physical relationship might have been open-ended, but our business one wasn't! You might think non-commitment is the be-all and end-all of things, but I don't! You've got financial and legal obligations to me, Flanagan,' she roared. 'And——'

The foul, four-letter expletive from Flanagan cut off her tirade mid-stream, but his sneering look of disgust as he stormed to the door upset her far more.

'It's always the money with you lot, isn't it? Geez, you're all the same! I wonder how much goddamn older I have to get before I wise up to the fact for once and for all?'

'Flan——'

'Stuff it, Jacqui! There's nothing more you can say in this lifetime that I'm interested in hearing!' In one vicious motion he slid open the glass door. 'I'll see you in court!'

His words seemed to reverberate with the glass as the door was dragged closed behind him.

No, you won't, Flanagan, she thought, making no effort even to remain standing much less to stem the tears streaming down her face. It was only a bluff. Even if I could afford to sue I wouldn't.

Two days later, as she loaded the washing machine and came across one of Flanagan's T-shirts, Jacqui again found herself fighting tears. Grasping the shirt to her breast, she inhaled the scent of him, wondering how long it would be before painful memories metamorphosed into the happy ones Caro had said they'd become.

Caro had tried hard to convince Jacqui that she was only imagining herself in love with Flanagan, but from where Jacqui stood her sister's theory—that real love was never one-sided—wasn't any more reliable than all the other platitudes. Whoever said that crying made you feel better were the world's biggest liars. Though they took the title only marginally ahead of the idiots who'd come up with, 'You'll feel better after a good night's sleep,' and, 'It's better to have loved and lost' et cetera!

They're all lies! Jacqui thought, willing herself to anger in an effort to ward off more tears. I've practically cried myself to dehydration and I still feel lousy! I can't get even a good hour's sleep because memories of *him* keep torturing my mind and body! And I'd give my right arm along with every internal organ to have never loved at all!

But, she told herself, mopping her eyes on his shirt, she wasn't crying because she wanted Flanagan back. *No*. She was crying because she was sick of being miserable and didn't want to love him any more. She wanted to *stop* feeling the way she did about him. She wanted to stop wondering if he was missing her or even thinking of her. If Flanagan didn't want *her*, why should she have to suffer being in love with *him*? What was the point of this agonising emptiness that enveloped her?

The worst thing about the pain of her heartbreak was that it touched every aspect of her life, contaminating things which hadn't even been a part of her time with Flanagan.

She couldn't laugh at Phil's jokes any more, or enjoy watching her niece and nephew cavort in the pool. She couldn't even feel relief, much less happiness, over Caro's announcement that the house *had* to be sold because Phil had received a promotion interstate and they'd need their half of the money to re-establish themselves. Even knowing that her own share would cover all but a few thousand of her father's outstanding debt wasn't sufficient to activate Jacqui's enthusiasm.

'Dammit, Flanagan!' she wailed. 'I could kill you for what you've done to me!' She looked at the tear-wet shirt she held, then hurled it across the room. 'And I'll be damned if I'll wash your rotten clothes!'

At least now she could get angry, she reasoned. That was a good sign. Dumping the rest of her things into the machine, she viciously switched it on. If anger was the only alternative to the aching loneliness she'd experienced over the last few days then she was going to stay angry! *Really* angry! And if, as her well-intentioned brother-in-law had claimed, time healed all wounds, then he'd better be able to tell her exactly what time! Because, as of now, she had no intention of being late!

Draped only in a towel, Patric picked up all the newspapers lying beneath the letter box in the front door and padded back down the hall into the kitchen. Gritting his teeth, he opened the blind and, after blinking in violent protest at the sun's morning brightness, he cast his blurry vision towards the empty Jack Daniels bottles lining the breakfast bar. He groaned. Eight.

God, he hoped he'd only averaged one a day. Of course, considering the hangover he was suffering, one an hour was a distinct possibility. Pouring himself a strong cup of percolated coffee, he counted the newspapers to collaborate his estimate. Five newspapers—a five-day drunk. Five days without Jacqui.

The coffee was bitter, but no more so than the knowledge that he'd fallen hopelessly in love while arrogantly thinking himself immune to such emotions. Now, though, he recognised that *that* had been his problem all along—thinking that his previous experience with Angel made him immune to Jacqui. The fact was that only *real* love had the power to immunise you against repeated outbreaks, and what he'd felt for Angel didn't even make a dent in the feelings he had for Jacqui.

Beautiful, sexy, funny, lovable Jacqui. Hell, he was still having trouble reconciling the image of what he'd believed her to be with the words she'd spoken the other morning, and the more he tried to the more it hurt. Dammit, he felt as if she'd totally gutted him. Sighing, he topped up his coffee-cup, but overfilled it as the sight of the countless photographs scattered across the floor of the studio caught his attention.

They represented both the posed and the candid shots he'd taken of her; he assumed that at some stage during the last alcohol-blurred few days he must have flung them from one end of the room to the other. In many ways he was only sorry that he hadn't burned them, because, sober, such sacrilege was beyond him. There was no doubt that they represented the best work he'd ever produced, but it was the content not the quality that made destroying them impossible.

Giving in to what he could only describe as a previously deep-seated masochistic streak, he started into the room and, setting the cup on the coffee-table, began picking them up one by one.

The unidentifiable anger he'd felt while developing the film had confused him at first, and it hadn't been until he'd awoken in Jacqui's bed the next morning that he'd recognised it for what it was: *jealousy*—a fiercely irrational wave of jealousy at the thought of sharing any part of her with other men, even only visually.

He'd told himself that he was being stupid, but, standing beneath the hot spray of her shower, he had been forced to admit the truth. He loved Jacqui. Totally and irrevocably.

He should probably have been grateful that he hadn't had the chance to make a complete idiot of himself and tell her. Except now, looking at her beautiful face smiling at him in glorious gut-wrenching detail from the close-up he held, he didn't feel grateful. He felt...well, he felt *loved*! Which only went to show that he was so far gone that he was imagining that a photograph of someone else could mirror his own feelings! He was a good photographer, but not even his old man had been that good!

Suddenly he reached for another photograph of Jacqui, then another and another. In a frenzy of hope he jumped up and snatched one of his father's portfolios from the floor-to-ceiling shelves and frantically fingered his way through it until he found a close-up shot of her done by Wade for Risque.

Still too afraid to believe what his eyes and gut were telling him, and suspicious of the soft-focus effect his father had used, he grabbed a more recently dated album, flipping hastily through it until he found what he was looking for—a clear, full-face blow-up of Jacqui. Holding his breath, he compared it to the shots he'd taken.

A raucous cheer broke from his throat as he leapt at the only conclusion that would satisfy him. He knew that he was grinning from ear to ear as he raced in to dress; he only prayed that on this occasion the camera hadn't lied!

Jacqui drove straight into the garage, hit the brake with more force than was necessary, and switched off the engine. Thank God she was home! she thought, releasing her seatbelt. She loathed the evening rush hour almost as much as she loathed snooty-nosed public servants and gossiping, opinionated hairdressers! And today had been wall to wall with all of them!

She picked up her handbag and the paper bag containing tonight's dinner and added another item to her list of loathsome things—fresh-faced schoolkids who worked in fast food drive-throughs and said, 'Enjoy your meal; have a nice evening!'

Because she knew that she wouldn't enjoy her meal or have a nice evening! Because these days everything she ate tasted like battery acid and tonight was going to be every bit as rotten and miserable as the last four——

'Jacqui!'

The excited shout coincided with her car door being wrenched open and herself being hauled from behind the wheel and entrapped against a hard male body. Fear made her heart pound at ten times its normal rate—fear that she was hallucinating and only imagining the sight, scent, sound and strength of Flanagan, as she'd done countless times during the last four lonely nights.

She lowered her eyelids against burning tears, telling herself that she was imagining his presence in the garage and that when she opened them again she'd be alone.

Pain and panic rose at the thought, yet she opened her eyes none the less.

She *wasn't* hallucinating! Flanagan was here—in her garage!

CHAPTER SIXTEEN

'FLANAGAN!' she screamed. 'Get out of my garage! Get out of my face! Get out of my life!'

'No.'

'No! What do you mean *no*?' she demanded, trying to shove his immoveable bulk away. 'It's *my* garage and *my* life!'

'And *your* face.' Her traitorous heart flipped as two large male hands lifted to her face and grazed her cheekbones in an achingly familiar fashion. 'Your beautiful, honest, open, loving face.' He smiled. 'And *that*, my beautiful, furious lady, is what I want to talk about.'

'Forget it, Flanagan!' she said, shaking her head. 'To quote you, "there's nothing more you can say in this lifetime that I'm interested in hearing"!'

'I was wrong. I made a mistake——'

'Me too!' she told him. 'And I'm not about to make another. Let me go!'

'I can't,' he whispered, his eyes closing as if a terrible pain was tearing at him. 'Oh, Jacqui, I can't. I *need* you.' He stepped closer, pinning her between the warmth of his body and the cool enamel of her car. Her mind told her to resist, but her heart was at the mercy of the strained, tired, but utterly dear face bending to hers.

'Oh, God,' he muttered, with a desperation she identified with. 'I've missed you...'

Please, Lord, she prayed, let him be real. Let *this* be real. Otherwise you might as well let me die now.

God's response was quick but confusing. For when moist male lips met hers her pulse reacted so violently that for an instant Jacqui thought she was in the throes of a fatal heart attack. But, after the initial desperation of the kiss had waned into a slow, gentle mating of tongues and nibbling of lips, she was convinced that she'd skipped death yet still reached heaven.

With Flanagan's hands eagerly reacquainting themselves with her body, physical bliss freed her from the mental anguish of the last few days. Weaving her fingers into his thick, collar-length hair, she sighingly surrendered to the dictates of her emotions.

Patric welcomed her kisses with a hunger only a starving man could have understood. He'd deprived himself of her sustenance for five long days, believing that man-made liquid could cure his hunger; now he knew that only the warm, womanly flesh pressing against him could fill his emptiness.

And such were his feelings for this woman that he doubted if he would ever have enough of her. Her kisses had the power to squeeze tears from his soul, yet at the same time lift him to the heights of ecstasy. He wanted her with the ferocity of an out-of-control bushfire, yet he wanted her with the gentle softness of her infant nephew he'd so recently held.

The groan that broke from his throat was a mixture of frustration and confusion. He felt as though he was being torn apart by two equally strong forces—the rough power of passion and the tender lure of love; for while his body was impatient to have access to the heated female one in his arms his heart was equally anxious to share itself with Jacqui.

When the need for oxygen finally separated them they were both trembling with desire, but Patric decided to gamble with his heart.

'Honey,' he said roughly, 'we've got to talk.'

Jacqui told herself not to read too much into what his presence here meant. It was no easy order, considering that she was a victim of kiss-impaired breathing and an intoxicating dose of hope and, just possibly, a complete emotional breakdown. Focusing on the toes of his trainers, she nodded.

His hand slipped under her hair to her chin, then pulled back as if burned. 'You've had your hair cut!'

His tone was enough to jerk her head up and at the same time make her wish that she'd never heard the word scissors. Cutting her hair had been a mistake! A pathetically symbolic attempt to sever all ties with her modelling career and get on with her life. Now, as Flanagan whimsically ran the fingers of both his hands through its new shoulder length, she cursed herself for not waiting one more day.

'I like it,' he said softly.

'You . . . you do?'

'How could I not?' He touched her cheek. 'It's *your* hair.' He barely gave her time to digest what he'd said before adding, 'But dammit, honey, it doesn't take all day to cut a person's hair, even when it's as long as yours was! I've been here nearly nine hours waiting for you! You've had me worried sick.'

'It shows, Flanagan,' she said, gazing up at his harried but endearingly handsome face. 'You look like hell.'

He groaned. 'Yeah. Well, to be honest, the bulk of the blame for that lies with Jack Daniels not Jacqui Raynor. I——'

'Jacqui *Raynomovski*,' she corrected. At his confused frown she explained, 'That's what I've been doing most of today—arranging to have my name legally changed back to Raynomovski.'

'Oh?' he said, directing an almost smug smile at her. 'Why?'

Distracted as much by the gleam in his eyes as by the way his body was brushing hers, it took her a moment to answer. 'Er—I've decided to quit modelling for good. Cutting my hair and going back to being plain old Jacqui Raynomovski seemed like a good way to start.'

'Would you have any problems with being plain old Jacqui Flanagan?'

Her heart stopped and she looked at him in utter disbelief. 'F-F-Flan——'

'I admit it doesn't roll off the tongue as easily as Raynomovski, but——'

'Flanagan,' she interrupted, 'are . . . are you . . . ?' Her thoughts scattered in the face of his gorgeous grin and the touch of his hands on her bare shoulders.

'Am I what?' he prompted, his hands now sliding down her arms.

'St-stop it, Flanagan,' she protested as her bones began to liquefy. 'I can't think.'

He released her and stepped back. 'I'd hoped it wouldn't be that hard a question to answer, Jacqui,' he said softly, his eyes and smile dimming.

'It isn't!' she assured him. 'It's just that . . . I need to know *exactly* what you mean. Are . . . are we talking long-term commitment here, or——' she swallowed hard '—or . . . or . . . ?' Annoyed with herself and him, she stamped her foot. 'Dammit, Flanagan, are you asking me to live with you or to marry you?'

He was obviously struggling to verbalise his thoughts, and with fear burning in her veins Jacqui wished she could have bitten off her tongue. She lowered her head to conceal her tears. Oh, God, she'd blown it again!

'I'm talking long-term commitment with a capital C and all the Ts crossed and the Is dotted.' Her head jerked up at the sound of his strong, clear voice, weighted with conviction. 'I love you, Jacqui—more than you'll ever know, a million times more than I'll probably ever be able to tell you. But marry me, and at least give me the rest of your life to try.'

'Oh, Flanagan, *yes*!' She threw herself at him and was caught firmly against his heart. 'Yes! Yes! Ye——' Her tearfully elated chant was cut off by his kiss, and it was a long time before either was interested in or capable of speaking.

'So,' he said, a smile twinkling in the brown depths of his eyes. 'Are you planning on admitting that *you* love *me* any time soon?'

'You *know* I love you!' she accused him.

'Say it, babe,' he urged. '*Tell* me. I need to *hear* it just once.'

'But I told you that morning, when we were making...' Her words faded in the face of his negatively shaking head. 'But I was sure I had. At least, I *thought* I had,' she qualified. 'I mean...I thought that was the reason you wanted to end the shoot.'

'Hon', I didn't want to publish the photographs because I didn't want to share you with anyone else. But when you brought up the money—well, I——'

'Flanagan,' Jacqui wailed, 'I'm not going to sue you! I don't care about the money! I never did. Well, I did— but not more than you. And I don't now—care about the money, I mean. Naturally I care about you! But I only agreed to posing nude in the first place because I had a debt the size of the budget deficit. But I don't now. Well, I mean, I do—but it'll be gone when the house sells, and——'

'Shh,' he said, chuckling. 'Phil and Caro told me everything.' He traced her bottom lip with his thumb.

'They...they did?'

'Well, everything except how you feel about me. On that score they were gambling on appearances—like I was.'

'Oh, Flanagan, you idiot,' she whispered. 'Of course I *love* you!'

She was swung into his arms and cradled tightly as he strode from the garage.

'Oh, God, honey,' he muttered into her neck. 'It seems like I've waited a lifetime to hear you say that. 'Course,' he chuckled, nipping her shoulder, 'in my version you left out the "idiot" bit!'

She laughed. 'You deserve it for what you've put me through the last five days!'

'If you think *that* was tough wait until you see what I've got lined up for the next few!' He wiggled his eyebrows.

'Sounds interesting,' she purred. 'Give me a clue.'

He grinned, deftly sliding her door open with his foot and carrying her inside.

'Well, first thing—after I've spent the next twelve or so hours making mad, passionate love to you—we're going out to get a marriage licence and a pool table. Then we're——'

She blinked as he lowered her on to her bed. 'Don't you mean a marriage licence and a *ring*?'

'Nope,' he said, putting his fingers into his pocket. 'I've already got one.'

He crouched beside the bed and, taking her left hand, gently kissed each finger until he came to her third. At that point he kissed the ring he held and slipped it on to her finger. Jacqui was helpless to control her tears as she looked down at the gold design of two hands clasping a heart.

'Oh, Flanagan,' she cried. 'It's beautiful.'

'It's a Claddagh ring—the traditional Irish wedding ring.' He kissed her softly, then rested his forehead against hers. 'It was my grandmother's, and I swear no one but her has ever worn it.'

Jacqui knew that his words were a subtle attempt to assure her that it had never been Angel's, that his *heart* had never truly been Angel's, and she smiled. There was just enough bitchiness in Jacqui for her to be smugly pleased.

'I love you, babe,' he said softly, and his kiss, as it tilted her backwards on to the mattress, reinforced his words.

Some hours later Patric opened his eyes and found himself looking into a pair of perplexed blue ones. Fear that something had happened to make her change her mind about marrying him ensured that he was instantly alert.

'What's up, babe?' he asked, his fingers instinctively trying to smooth her frown.

'Flanagan, why do we have to buy a *pool table*? If you've got the urge for snooker we could just go to the local pub——'

His relief was so enormous that he nearly tumbled them on to the floor as he lunged at her. Oh, God, he loved this woman! Even more incredibly, she loved him!

'You don't want a pool table?' he asked innocently as she hung half off the bed.

'Well, to be honest, I've never really thought about it.'

'I have,' he smirked. 'And not having one has nearly killed me.'

She blinked. 'Well, if you like snooker *that* much—get one.' She smiled. 'It's not as if your game couldn't use the practice!'

Grinning, he trailed a slow hand over her hip. 'Oh, it's not the idea of playing snooker that appeals to me.'

'It's...it's not?'

'Uh-uh. Ever since that night at the pub I've fantasised about having you naked and writhing beneath me on green felt.'

A red blush rose in her face and he frowned. 'Too kinky for you, huh?'

She shook her head, her nails grazing the skin of his chest. 'Nope, Flanagan.' She grinned. 'But we'd *really* have been on dangerous ground if you'd been able to read my mind *that* night—'cause we were definitely on the same wavelength!'

Her words and the look of desire in her blue eyes sent his heart and blood racing. 'Ah, hell, lady, I think I'm going to die loving you!'

She slipped her arms around his neck and pulled his head down. 'My thoughts *exactly*, Flanagan!'

EPILOGUE

THREE years later Jacqui opened the door of her riverside Cabarita home and was immediately hugged by her very pregnant sister, then Phil, her two nephews, and finally her niece.

'C'mon through,' she managed, when the hugs and kisses were out of the way. 'Flanagan's out in the studio doing another bear rug layout.'

'Oh?' Caro raised an inquisitive eyebrow. 'I thought he was busy putting together an exhibition of Flanagan Photographs—his, yours and Wade's?'

'He is.' Jacqui smiled, opening the folding timber doors and revealing her husband, crouched with camera poised, next to where their nappy-clad, raven-haired eighteen-month-old twin daughters were sprawled on fleecy sheepskins.

'I hate to tell you this, mate,' Phil said in hushed tones, 'but they're *sleeping*, not posing.'

Lowering the camera, Flanagan grinned and crossed the room. 'And I thought you were an amateur,' he joked, shaking his brother-in-law's hand. 'How was the drive up from Melbourne?'

'Mummy, you said we could have a drink when we got to Aunty Jac's,' Simone complained.

'Yeah! You said!' her younger brothers echoed.

Caro rolled her eyes. 'We've got three kids and another due in a couple of months and you have to *ask*, Patric.'

'Beats me how you haven't worked out what's causing them yet,' he said drily, scooping the youngest boy into his arms. 'C'mon, let's see what goodies we've got in our fridge, huh?'

As the crowd trooped to the kitchen Jacqui tiptoed over and placed a light sheet over the sleeping Siobhan and Deirdre, her heart lifting at the sight of their chubby faces serene in sleep. Awake, they were such a noisy, mischievous handful that Flanagan had nicknamed them Search and Destroy, but Jacqui couldn't have loved them more if she'd tried—nor, she knew, could their father. She remembered the day she'd told him she was pregnant, and the glorious joy which had filled Flanagan's face . . .

'You're . . . you're sure?' he'd asked. 'Really sure?'

She'd laughed. 'Yes, Flanagan, I'm *sure*! Doubly sure. In fact I'm having twins.'

'*Two*?'

'Your fault, Flanagan. You're the one with twins in the family.'

'*Two*.' He'd shaken his head, bemused. 'I don't know much about fathering *one*——'

'You'll do fine,' she'd promised laughingly. 'Better than fine! God's giving you two because He *knows* you're going to be a *wonderful* dad.'

'I'm just glad He gave me *you*,' he'd said softly. 'Because it means our children will have the one thing I want most for them—a mother who'll love, nurture and care for them, and never, ever make them feel like an inconvenience.' He'd lowered his head then, and reverently kissed her flat abdomen before lifting her into his arms. 'I love you, Jacqui. More than anything in this world, I love you . . .'

Sounds of laughter coming from the kitchen pulled her from her recollections and, dropping a kiss on each of the sleeping toddlers, she went to join the others.

The kids were charging around the yard in safe view of the adults sitting on the patio.

'Did you pour me a drink, Flanagan?' she asked, perching on the arm of his chair.

'Gee, *Patric*,' Caro said, shaking her head, 'three years of marriage and you still can't get her to call you by your first name.'

'I do sometimes,' Jacqui responded slyly.

'Yeah,' her husband agreed, handing her a glass of wine and smiling up at her with a loving look she'd never tire of. 'But you'd never believe how hard I have to work to get her to do it!'

MILLS & BOON

Just Married

Celebrate the joy, excitement and adjustment that comes with being 'Just Married' in this wonderful collection of four new short stories.

Written by four popular authors

Sandra Canfield

Muriel Jensen

Elise Title

Rebecca Winters

Just Married is guaranteed to melt your hearts— just married or not!

Available: April 1996   Price: £4.99

MILLS & BOON

Today's Woman

Mills & Boon brings you a new series of seven
fantastic romances by some of your favourite
authors. One for every day of the week in fact
and each featuring a truly wonderful woman
who's story fits the lines of the old rhyme
'Monday's child is...'

Look out for Patricia Knoll's
Desperately Seeking Annie in April '96.

Thursday's child Annie Parker is recovering
from amnesia when she meets a tall dark
handsome stranger who claims to be her
husband. But how can she spend the rest of her
life with a man she can't even remember—
let alone remember marrying?

Temptation

Coming up in
BACHELOR ARMS...

When Blythe Fielding planned her wedding and asked her two best friends, Caitlin and Lily, to be bridesmaids, none of them had a clue a new romance was around the corner for each of them—even the bride!

These entertaining, dramatic stories of friendship, mystery and love by **JoAnn Ross** continue to follow the exploits of the residents of Bachelor Arms. If you loved the male Bachelor Arms titles you'll love the next set coming up in Temptation featuring the female residents of this lively apartment block.

Look out for:

FOR RICHER OR POORER (March 1996)
THREE GROOMS AND A WEDDING (April 1996)

GET 4 BOOKS
AND A MYSTERY GIFT

Return this coupon and we'll send you 4 Mills & Boon Romances and a mystery gift absolutely FREE! We'll even pay the postage and packing for you.

We're making you this offer to introduce you to the benefits of Reader Service: FREE home delivery of brand-new Mills & Boon romances, at least a month before they are available in the shops, FREE gifts and a monthly Newsletter packed with information.

Accepting these FREE books and gift places you under no obligation to buy, you may cancel at any time, even after receiving just your free shipment. Simply complete the coupon below and send it to:

MILLS & BOON READER SERVICE, FREEPOST, CROYDON, SURREY, CR9 3WZ.

No stamp needed

Yes, please send me 4 free Mills & Boon Romances and a mystery gift. I understand that unless you hear from me, I will receive 6 superb new titles every month for just £2.10* each postage and packing free. I am under no obligation to purchase any books and I may cancel or suspend my subscription at any time, but the free books and gifts will be mine to keep in any case. (I am over 18 years of age)

1EP6R

Ms/Mrs/Miss/Mr _____

Address _____

_____

_____ Postcode _____

mps MAILING PREFERENCE SERVICE

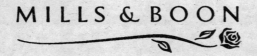

MILLS & BOON

Next Month's Romances

Each month you can choose from a wide variety of romance with Mills & Boon. Below are the new titles to look out for next month.

HOT BLOOD	Charlotte Lamb
PRISONER OF PASSION	Lynne Graham
A WIFE IN WAITING	Jessica Steele
A WOMAN TO REMEMBER	Miranda Lee
SPRING BRIDE	Sandra Marton
DESPERATELY SEEKING ANNIE	Patricia Knoll
THE BACHELOR CHASE	Emma Richmond
TAMING A TYCOON	Leigh Michaels
PASSION WITH INTENT	Natalie Fox
RUTHLESS!	Lee Wilkinson
MY HERO	Debbie Macomber
UNDERCOVER LOVER	Heather Allison
REBEL BRIDE	Sally Carr
SECRET COURTSHIP	Grace Green
PERFECT STRANGERS	Laura Martin
HEART'S REFUGE	Quinn Wilder